WHAT

LOVE

LOOKS

LIKE

JARLATH GREGORY is from Crossmaglen, County Armagh, and now lives in Stoneybatter, Dublin. He studied at Trinity College Dublin and is the author of the novels *Snapshots*, *G.A.A.Y* and *The Organised Criminal*.

WHAT

sometimes, love turns up ...

LOVE

LOOKS

... where you least expect it

LIKE

JARLATH GREGORY

THE O'BRIEN PRESS

DUBLIN

First published 2021 by
The O'Brien Press Ltd,
12 Terenure Road East, Rathgar,
Dublin 6, D06 HD27, Ireland.

Tel: +353 1 4923333; Fax: +353 1 4922777
E-mail: books@obrien.ie.
Website: www.obrien.ie
The O'Brien Press is a member of Publishing Ireland.

ISBN: 978-1-78849-162-4
Text © copyright Jarlath Gregory 2021
Copyright for typesetting, layout, editing, design
© The O'Brien Press Ltd
Design and layout by Emma Byrne
Cover image © Shutterstock

1 3 5 7 8 6 4 2
21 23 25 24 22

Printed in the UK by Clays Ltd, Elcograf S.p.A.
The paper in this book is produced using pulp from managed forests.

Published in

DUBLIN

UNESCO
City of Literature

This book is dedicated to

Colin Crummy, with fond

memories of our teenage selves

01

THE BIG DATE

When Ireland voted to let gay people get married, my stepdad hugged me and said, 'Your turn next, Ben! Get yourself a boyfriend. Make us proud.' So, I decided to try, because the time felt right. I was seventeen. I'd skipped Transition Year, flown through my Leaving Cert and was taking a year out to do work experience in the local primary school, before going on to do teacher training. And now, I was ready to start dating. I had a smartphone, I had some money and I wasn't too ugly. What more did you need?

It was three weeks later, Friday night, and I'd started looking. I was walking home in the lashing rain, and I didn't even care. I'd just been on the best date ever. The fact that we hadn't even kissed, never mind slept together, only made it more romantic. The lampposts dripped with rain. Cars sped past. Dublin buses swayed gently from side to side. People scurried by with their collars turned up, under umbrellas, as the rain bounced off the pavement and splashed up their legs. I always keep my head shaved and my collar buttoned up, and even though my toes were squelching in my trainers, I couldn't keep the grin off my face. I'd decided to walk home instead of getting the bus because, like the sappy heroine of some crappy old book you're forced to read in English class, even the weather couldn't get me down. Someone's granny peered at me suspiciously, as if I must be mad to be smiling through the torrential downpour, but she hadn't been out drinking with a sexy Northern Irish lad called Peter, so I forgave her.

Peter and I met online, as you do. Before I tried it, I had the idea that online dating was slutty, but what's the alternative? Even though I love going out and dancing all night in gay bars, how many guys met their future husband when they were both dancing off their heads to Lady Gaga? Anyway, I guess online dating is only as slutty as the person doing it. Flashing your mickey all over the internet will probably get you noticed, but you're not really advertising yourself as boyfriend material, are you?

I'd explained this theory to my best gay pal, Soda, one night in the pub. He thought I was nuts.

'Girl,' Soda said (he calls everyone girl, mickeys or not), 'first of all, there's no such thing as a slut. Slut is just a horrible word that men use to put women down. You're either sexually liberated or practically a virgin, and you,' he continued, picking up my bottle of beer and pausing long enough to suck on it suggestively, 'are living a life of self-appointed celibacy. Seriously. How many boyfriends have you had, Ben?'

'Um,' I said.

'Can't hear you,' Soda said, wiping my beer off his glossy lips.

'None,' I said. Was that normal? I'd been with a few guys, sure, but I'd been waiting for the right time to date seriously. People like Soda seemed born ready.

'And I've had six, even though we're practically the same age! I mean, what are you waiting for? A dowry? Come on, you're seventeen already.'

'But you're a little bit older –'

'Shush,' Soda said, putting a nail-polished finger to my lips. 'You're legal. Get out there and get some action while you're still horny enough to lower your standards. Just think, once you're at college, you'll be looking for a husband. By the time you graduate, you'll be working on your career. Then you'll be stuck in a dreary teaching job, and your only fun in life will be an unrequited crush on one of the dads. Next thing you know, you'll be thirty. Gay death.'

I took a deep breath and tried to think of a polite way to

explain that not everyone was horny all the time, and besides, thirty was a lifetime away.

'But Soda, aren't you almost –?'

'Stop talking! I'm a perfectly respectable twenty-four years old, with years of wisdom and experience to pass on to the younger generation.'

'Even though your Grindr profile says twenty-two?' I said.

'You have to update it manually,' Soda said with dignity, 'and I've been busy. Look, once you hit thirty, you'll be sexually invisible for your remaining time on this planet. Fact of life. You might be cute, but it's not going to last, so start looking now, before it's too late. It's different for me. I'm half Japanese, so I only age at half the rate of you poor white boys. Remember, no guy'll marry you if you're rubbish in bed, so put yourself out there, take some portraits without pants, and worry about the lovey-dovey stuff later.'

Sometimes, it wasn't worth arguing with Soda.

'So, I just have to pretend to be over eighteen and try to filter out the dirty old men?'

'Exactly. You'll take the photos for him, Chelsea, won't you?'

Chelsea was my best friend, the same age as me but still at school. Luckily, Soda had taught us how to confidently walk into bars like we were eighteen already.

'Suck my dick, Soda,' Chelsea said. 'Whose round is it?'

'Ladylike as ever. I learned all my drag moves from you, girl.'

'Never mind sucking dick,' I said gloomily, 'I'd settle for a bag of chips and a snog on the way home.' I heaved myself up to get another round in. It helps that I've been shaving since I was fifteen, and Soda's cousin is good for fake IDs.

Well, back on the night of the big date, I didn't get a bag of chips or a snog on the way home, but I did get to hang out for a couple of hours with the most beautiful man I'd ever seen. I'd never really thought men could be beautiful, but this one definitely was. I was nervous as hell because you never know if someone's photos on their profile will match their face in real life, or whether Instagram filters have done all the hard work. There I was, sitting on my own, nervously texting Soda, saying how maybe I'd turned up too early, or got the wrong bar because all straight pubs kind of look the same, when Peter – the same Peter as his profile pics – appeared at my table, thrusting a big manly hand in my face.

I half stood up, nearly knocked over my beer, dropped my phone, half sat down, then thrust my hand out and grabbed his, shaking it in what I hoped was a masculine sort of way, and not like the sweaty, awkward mess I was turning into.

'Ben?'

'Hi, Peter. Yep. I'm always this clumsy. Sorry.'

'Better get your phone.' Peter winked at me as he shrugged

off his leather jacket. 'Your girlfriend will be wondering where you've got to.'

'He's not my – huh?'

It was one of those pubs full of locals, where the men and women sit in silence with the telly blaring. A dog yawned at the bar. Its owner tossed it half a bacon sandwich. Peter was tall and pale, with dark hair, a little bit of scruffy stubble, chiselled features and bright blue eyes. His voice had that north of the border twang, like he wanted to whisper something dirty in my ear.

We talked about ordinary stuff, like the estate I grew up in, how long he'd been in Dublin, his day job versus his career, the work experience I was doing now and my plans for college. When we left the bar – 'I really want to see you again, yeah?' – he punched my arm and smiled before he walked off, even though I wanted him to kiss me. I knew he wouldn't, not outside a pub with an old man in a flat cap sucking on a smelly pipe, not while someone was murdering Van Morrison's 'Brown Eyed Girl' at the amateur karaoke night, not when a gaggle of drunk women were laughing as one of their gang puked into the gutter. The whole time we were talking, the ugly look of the pub had melted away. It was only in small moments – when I saw the young Polish barman look us up and down with a bit of a sneer, or the way a smartly dressed woman smirked when she whispered something about us behind her hand to a friend, or when Peter leaned in to laugh at something and I wanted to take his face in my hands and kiss him on the lips – that I'd remembered how in lots of places, two boys still couldn't kiss each other and not ask for trouble.

Still, he'd been clear about what he wanted – *a discreet meet,* to see if we liked each other. *One pint, just to say hi.* Two pints if we got on, but he'd have to go home after that even if we liked each other, because he had work in the morning, and besides, *I don't do anonymous, you know?*

I did know, and I liked how we agreed about it. We'd had two pints, and that was a good sign. I watched Peter's back disappear into the crowd of people waiting to cross at the traffic lights and broke into a grin. I could barely remember what we'd talked about, but I did remember the way his eyes lit up when he laughed, and how he ran his fingers through his hair when he was thinking about something, and the way his short-sleeved checked shirt bit into his biceps. I resisted the urge to text him straight away. That was the kind of thing irritating girls did on TV, and it always got them dumped before a potential romance blossomed. I wondered if it would be safe to text him the next day. I'd have to ask Soda. He'd been born with an innate knowledge of the Rules of Dating (and How to Wear Make-up).

Walking home, I passed three girls shivering outside Centra, clutching fivers and tugging on their tiny skirts, trying to cover the bits between their knee-high boots and their underwear. They looked about fifteen, and were trying to persuade grown-ups to go inside and buy booze for them. The tallest was sucking on a cigarette, her eyes ringed with mascara like a raccoon. I looked older than I really was, so I kept my head down. They were too young for getting drunk outdoors on their own.

'Will you buy us a pack of Smirnoff Ice, mister?'

'You've got a piece of tobacco stuck in your braces,' I said, and walked on.

'Faggot!' she shouted after me.

See, here's the thing about the word faggot. First time someone calls you a faggot, you get upset because you feel like you did something wrong. After that, you learn to start hiding all the things about yourself that make you a faggot. And it's only later, when you find out that your real friends don't care how gay you are and that your family still loves you, that someone shouting 'faggot' at you in the street doesn't hurt as much, and you can walk away with your head held high. It still stings, though, no matter how many times you hear it. I wondered if she'd seen me leave the pub with Peter, and what he would say if he knew that kids could tell I was gay.

'I'm not really into, you know ...' he'd said in the pub, in a quiet voice. I'd leaned in closer, liking the way his stubble sort of framed his lips. 'The gay scene.'

'Oh, right. Cool.'

'It's all a bit …'

He'd waved his hand around, and I was reminded of Soda after three bottles of beer, but nodded anyway because I knew what he meant.

'Camp?'

'It's not really me, that's all.'

'Fair enough.' I wasn't sure how I felt about that, but his forearms were muscular and hairy, and my hand and my heart were already aching from his grasp, so I gave him the benefit of the doubt. 'Hey, what do you think's going to happen on *Game of Thrones?*'

Halfway home, the first few drops of rain fell on my face, cold and sharp. I shook off the feeling of being annoyed with the girl outside Centra. I looked up at the sky, all cloudy and grey, and knew it was going to spill. I stuck my hands in my pockets and rearranged my hard-on so I could walk properly in my skinny jeans, but that just made me grin some more. The rain splished and splashed and then began to bucket, but I didn't have a jacket, or a cap, or the money for a taxi, so I just kept on walking.

So there I was, on a bit of a beer buzz, horny and happy and wondering what it would feel like to be wrapped in Peter's arms, his breath on my neck, his legs around mine as we tussled on the bed, that cheeky accent in my ear as he whispered –

Sploosh!

A car sped around the corner and drenched my legs even more than they already were. I didn't care. I was nearly home. I picked up my pace, jogging through the shallow puddles on the pavement and kicking an old tin can, just because I could. It landed with a plop in a yellow plastic bucket that one of the kids on the estate had left outside.

Goal!

I felt invincible.

I stopped, yawned and stretched in the rain. I looked up at the sky and stuck my tongue out to catch some raindrops on it. Then I ran a hand over my scalp, shook the drops of water from my face and headed on to our house. I grew up in an estate on the northside of Dublin that everyone says is shit poor, but I like it. Yeah, so there's the odd broken-down car on someone's front lawn, and half our neighbours live on benefits, but so what? It's pretty much live and let live around here.

When I got to the gate, our house was more or less the same as usual. The grass in the front garden needed a trim. One of the light bulbs had blown on the porch. The front door needed a lick of paint. One thing was different though.

Someone had painted 'GAYS OUT' on our wall.

OK, so not everyone voted to let gay people get married. You still get the odd dickhead ruining it for everyone else. I knew which particular dickhead had done this, and I was going to kick his arse, but that could wait till tomorrow. I lingered on the doorstep, not ready to go inside just yet. A light came on in an upstairs window of the house next door. A familiar tousled head peeked out, a cigarette between its lips. Chelsea flipped on her lighter, which lit her face from below like a villain in a black and white movie. She's a big girl, but you'd never call her butch. She might punch your lights out.

We've been best friends since my family moved here, nine years ago. We met on the day I moved in. Me and Chelsea had drawn our water pistols over the dividing line of our shared garden wall. We'd sized each other up, lowered our guns and spent the rest of the day bitching about all the things that eight-year-olds hate.

'How was the big date?' Chelsea asked from the windowsill, blowing a lungful of smoke through the rain, which was easing off now I'd made it home, already drenched.

'Shouldn't you be studying?' I said.

'I can't be bothered,' Chelsea said, taking another drag. 'If I don't know the cosine of pi squared by now, I never will. Anyway, I've got a couple of weeks left to cram.'

'Good luck with that. Were you waiting up for me?'

'Don't flatter yourself. Smoking is my boyfriend. And I can't help noticing you're avoiding my question.'

It was true. Part of me wanted to hug the big date all to myself for a little bit longer. But I never kept anything from Chelsea, and she seemed more interested in my love life than the Leaving Cert. 'It was brilliant.'

'Oh yeah? Tell me everything.'

I had to take a deep breath because everything about Peter seemed amazing. Then the words came out all at once without me even having time to think.

'His name is Peter, he's nineteen and he's dead nice. Northern Irish. Works in a phone shop, but he really wants to be a photographer, or do his own podcast, or something like that, as long as it's in media. He's got a cheeky smile and amazing arms and he made me laugh. I wanted to grab his face and kiss him right there in the pub.'

Chelsea stopped loving her cigarette real hard. 'You didn't kiss him?'

I hesitated, feeling awkward. 'Well, no.'

'Did he kiss you?'

'He couldn't, could he?'

'And why not?'

'We were in a straight pub.'

I knew we were getting to the difficult part when Chelsea stubbed her cigarette out on the windowsill and flicked the butt all the way across the garden and over the wall. It bounced at my feet. The rain died off. I stood there all wet, the air smelling like freshly washed grass. Tiny beads of rain trickled down my face and neck.

'Why,' Chelsea asked, in a voice that could freeze your vodka martini at ten paces, 'were you in a straight pub, exactly?'

I stuck my hands in my pockets. The ground looked really interesting all of a sudden. 'Why shouldn't two gay guys go to a straight bar?' I sounded defensive, even to myself.

'Eh, so you can actually wear the face off each other on a first date? You mightn't get a smack in the mouth these days, but you're still going to get some funny looks.'

I stubbed my toe into the ground, thinking that I'd have to stuff my trainers with newspaper and leave them on the radiator to dry before bed.

'He's not out,' I mumbled.

'Did I hear that correctly?'

'He's not out!' I yelled.

'Uh huh. Yeah. I'll talk to you tomorrow,' Chelsea said, which somehow sounded like a threat. She popped her head back inside and shut the window with a bang.

Girls are so moody. When they talk about guys you have to

ask about her feelings and his feelings and what everyone else is going to think, and when you want to talk about two guys on a date, they don't get it anyway. Sometimes, I feel sorry for straight lads.

Anyway, I told myself, fishing my door key out of my pocket, my hard-on for Peter still threatening to poke a hole in my jeans, why shouldn't a fella stay in the closet if he wanted to? Life didn't have to be all drag queens and glitter and vodka martinis. Maybe if you wanted a proper boyfriend, a real man to hold you, you had to steer clear of the scene – right?

I got the key in the door on the third attempt, which made me think about sex, and that made me giggle. I was probably more drunk than I realised. Oops. I wiped my feet on the mat, trying to be quiet, and knocked over the umbrella stand. I'd always thought umbrella stands were daft pieces of furniture, but now that I was soaking wet, crawling on my hands and knees to find the scattered umbrellas, I saw them in a whole new light. They suddenly seemed like the best idea in the world. I was just warming to the idea of being a grown-up, smugly carrying an umbrella while everyone else got wet, when my stepdad appeared on the landing, gripping a golf club.

I grinned up at him, trying my best to look sober.

'Oh, hey. Thought you were burglars. How was the big date?'

'Did Mum tell you?'

'Of course she told me. She said you were dead excited.'

I stood up and brushed my knees off, trying to be all dignified, but failing. 'It was good, yeah.'

'That's my boy. Don't let him know how much you like him. You have to play a bit hard to get. Don't go jumping into –'

'Nathan!' Look, Nathan means well and everything, but I was saving all my embarrassing dating questions for Soda. And even then, I'd need a few more drinks.

'I know, I know. I'll shut up now. Night-night. Don't forget to put the umbrellas back and turn the lights off, yeah?'

'Nathan?'

'Yeah?'

'Did you see the graffiti outside?'

Nathan nodded. 'I'm sorry you had to see that, Ben. I got home too late to clean it off tonight, but I'll do it first thing in the morning.' Nathan relaxed his grip on the golf club. He never gets angry, but he does get disappointed. 'Stupid little sods. If I knew who wrote that, I'd march right round to their house and ask their parents if they were proud of what their kids turned out like.'

Nathan's family are Jamaican. After my mum and dad split up, she met Nathan, and then my little sister came along. When the divorce came through, Mum and Nathan got married, and we moved here to get away from reminders of Mum's old life.

We used to get some funny looks – white mum, black dad, one white son, one mixed-race daughter – but Mum always said we shouldn't care what other people thought. Besides, Nathan is more of a dad to me than my real dad ever was. I still called him Nathan, though. I've never met his mum and dad – they're still in Jamaica – but sometimes we talk to each other on Skype. My granny and granddad took a long time to get used to the idea that their daughter separated from my dad, had a mixed-race kid, got divorced and married a black man, but the more they got to know Nathan, the more they softened, little by little.

'I'll take care of it,' I said.

Nathan nodded and went back to bed. He trusts me. We're cool. I dried myself off, remembered to dry out my trainers too and put myself to bed. My room was cosy and warm after getting caught in the rain. Mum had put new bedsheets on, and the pillows were nice and fluffy. I lay back and reached for the tissues on my bedside table. I was settling in, thinking of Peter's arms, legs, face, everything, when my phone buzzed.

One hand down my boxers and the other on my phone, I thought it might be Peter texting to say goodnight – but no. It was only Soda. Typical.

So? How was the big date?

I politely took my hand out of my boxers to reply.

I think he might be the one!

02

BOYS AND BOXERS

Next morning, I stormed over to Aaron McAnally's house. It was an end-of-terrace house with a big garden near the bus stop. It looked like something out of an ad for sofas, or car insurance, or muesli. His parents were into home improvements, Mass and looking down their noses at everybody else. Aaron had been a year ahead of me at school. He used to steal my schoolbag and throw it onto the roof of the bike sheds, call me a 'gay boy' on the bus, or wait for me after school to shove me up against a wall and ask if I wanted a kiss, while all his mates laughed, like boys kissing boys was the funniest thing in the world. But I was on top of my work, and I wanted to be a teacher, so I decided to skip Transition Year and finish my Leaving Cert a year early. The only downside was that for the last two years at school I was in the same class as Aaron. I almost didn't skip ahead just to avoid him, but Nathan said I shouldn't let him hold me back, and he was right. Mum said if I really wanted to be a teacher, she'd get me work experience in her school if I got enough points for teacher training, before starting college with people my own age. That had settled it. But even now, the things that Aaron had done still stung.

On my first day in Fifth Year, Aaron put up his hand in religion class and asked the teacher about the Catholic Church's view on gay marriage. He looked at me with a big grin on his face as the teacher explained how gay marriage was against God's plan and all that stuff. I turned bright red and wanted to fall through the floor, but then, one by one, the other kids started to stick up for gay people. OK, so it usually started with, 'I'm not gay, but ...' but at least it showed Aaron that he couldn't say whatever he wanted and get away with it. I learned to keep my head down, ignore him and get the grades I needed. I kept telling myself it would be worth it, and besides, I still hung out with Chelsea after school. I would be starting college next September, but Aaron either didn't get the points for college or didn't want to go. As luck would have it, he got a job as a gardener in the school where Mum worked and I was doing my work experience, so I still had to see him now and then.

I usually kept out of his way, but this time, he'd gone too far.

The McAnallys' garden looked perfect, as always, but Aaron still had a 'Vote No!' poster stuck up inside his bedroom window from the gay marriage referendum, as if his side hadn't lost. Aaron was lying back on a plastic sun lounger, sunbathing topless. His boxer dog was sitting on his chest, as usual. His best friends, Darren and Wayne, were sitting either side of him in the grass, drinking cans of beer. I hopped over the white wooden gate, which annoyed the boxer dog. She jumped off Aaron's chest and came bounding over, drooling and yapping at me. It wasn't her fault she belonged to such a horrible person, so I crouched down to tickle behind her ears.

'Oi! Killer! Get away from the gay boy,' Aaron yelled. 'You might get dog AIDS.'

'Do dogs get AIDS?' Darren said.

'I dunno,' Wayne said, 'but all your girlfriends are dogs.'

I stood up as tall as I could, fists clenching, that familiar tingle of fear rising in my belly. This wasn't school, I told myself. I could do this. 'I know you graffitied our wall,' I said, hoping my voice didn't sound too shaky or too gay. 'Next time, I'll get the cops on you.'

'Oh yeah? Good luck with that. You don't have any proof.'

'They'll soon find proof. You're not that smart.' My jaw was clenching too. It was hard to get the words out. 'I bet someone around here saw you do it. Your mum and dad might let you away with it, but I won't.'

I was breathing hard. Aaron stood up and walked towards me slowly, as Darren took a slurp from his can and Wayne gawped. Killer jumped up and down at Aaron's feet, but he ignored her. He walked up close to me, put a hand on my chest and stuck his face right into mine. His brown hair was cut in a blunt fringe, and there was pink sunburn on his nose and forehead. He'd got more muscular from all the gardening. I tried not to look at his naked chest, or the place where his sun cream hadn't been rubbed in properly on his shoulder, or the trail of hair leading up to his belly button. OK, it would've been a tiny bit sexy if it had been literally anyone else. I forced myself to look at his face. We were the same height, but the way he stood in front of me made me feel small.

'Shove off,' he said. 'You're on my property and I want you to leave.'

'*Woof!*' said Killer.

'You can say what you like to my face,' I said. 'I'm a grown-up. I can take it. But if you graffiti our house, you're bringing my family into it. My family are off limits, do you hear me? Leave them out of it.' It was only after I'd said it out loud that I knew it was true. Something had changed since school. Me.

Aaron picked Killer up off the ground, nuzzling her into his chest. He kissed her slobbery face, then scratched her head, making swirly patterns on the crown of the dog's skull. 'Your family? Don't make me laugh. Do you know what your family are?'

I could feel my face go red.

'Your family are fucking mongrels. Divorced, remarried, half black, with a gay boy. Your family is everything that's wrong with this country. But right now, you're the one that's pissing me off the most. Why don't you go home to your kennel? That place you call home isn't fit for my dog.'

With a quick, hard push that took me by surprise, Aaron sent me sprawling into the garden. The world was spinning. I didn't even have time to feel sore.

'And get off my lawn!'

Darren and Wayne burst out laughing. 'Is the little gay boy crying?'

'Need a hand chucking him out?'

'Don't let the garden gate smack you on the arse, gay boy,' Aaron said. 'You might like it.'

They all thought that was pretty funny.

I swallowed my anger. Some of the neighbours were staring. You have to act better than the people who yell stuff at you in the street because, otherwise, when you yell back, when you lose the head or get mad, the same people will say you were asking for it. They all like to stare but they never speak up for you. There was nothing I could do, so I got up and let myself out through the gate – my arse was too sore to hop over it – trying not to hobble.

'Oh yeah,' Aaron called as I walked away, trying not to look like I was in pain, 'and keep your faggoty eyes off me in future.'

I stopped and turned back. 'What are you talking about?'

'I saw the way you were looking at my body,' Aaron said, flexing for a horde of imaginary admirers, 'but this hot body's not for faggots, right?'

I felt ashamed, because it was kind of true, so it was easier to say nothing.

And with that, Aaron threw himself down on his sun lounger, as Darren and Wayne scrabbled to get him a beer and Killer growled at me from beyond the gate.

I felt a bit shittier as I walked home, face to the pavement, rubbing my tailbone better. I tried to think about all the stuff I liked about Ireland to cheer myself up, like chip shops and Chinese takeaways, drinking in the park or getting shushed by your mum when she's catching up with *Coronation Street* on Sunday, secretly guilty about not going to Mass. And it was cool when boys played football with rolled-up jumpers for goalposts and girls practised dance moves in the street – and if some of the girls and boys wanted to swap places, that was cool too. But there was another Ireland I didn't like, where people made fun of Jamie's hair, or hated the foreigners who did the jobs Irish people didn't want, where gay teachers still couldn't come out in case they lost their jobs.

I wanted to be a teacher. I wanted to be out. I wanted to be the out, proud gay teacher I didn't have when I was growing up. I wanted kids to know it was OK to be different, and who cared what some smelly old pope said anyway?

'Religion,' Soda said once, spraying enough hairspray on his wig to blow a new hole in the ozone layer, 'is just a fairy tale for grown-ups.'

Well, so much for Saturday morning. Back home, Nathan was on his hands and knees, scrubbing the graffiti off our wall with a bucket and a rag.

'Here, let me help.'

Nathan tossed me a sponge.

We worked in silence for a few minutes. The paint began to dissolve, but the wall would still have to be repainted when we finished. It didn't mean the words would go away. And what would stop Aaron, or anyone else, doing it again? It wasn't like I had a gang of people to stand up for me. I wrung out the sponge, dipped it in the bucket of water, and kept scrubbing. Saturday began to brighten up, crisp and clear after last night's rain. I tried to think about more good things – the cinnamon rolls and bacon Mum was making for breakfast, going back to work next week and seeing the kids I was helping at school, the way the hair swept across Peter's arms – but it wasn't much use.

'Don't let them get you down, son,' Nathan said. I flinched involuntarily but tried not to let it show, like I always did when Nathan called me 'son'. I pretended not to find it weird, so as not to hurt his feelings. It was easier not to think about my real dad, wherever he was.

There were things I remembered about my real dad, like the way he always smelled of cigarette smoke, or how his hand shook when he poured the tea, or how he sometimes fell asleep on the sofa in the middle of the day, which I didn't understand back then. Sometimes I was tempted to try and find out what he was doing now. Did he have a job, or was he in prison, or maybe drying out in rehab again? But most of the time, I was happy Mum had left him. After all, Mum and Nathan were happier together, and Jamie wouldn't be here if they'd never met.

It was just a shame that my real dad was such a waster.

Whatever happened, I didn't want to be like him.

Nathan's voice brought me back into the moment. 'Look, you get dickheads everywhere. Just imagine how small their lives are if just the fact that you exist can piss them off.'

I concentrated really hard on scrubbing off the letter A. 'Yeah,' I said.

Nathan stopped scrubbing at the wall. 'So you know who it was?'

The paint was stubborn. I couldn't get it to shift. 'Aaron McAnally.'

Our hands were hovering over the graffiti, mine over 'GAYS' and Nathan's over 'OUT'. Nathan looked at me in surprise, then his face hardened, and he squeezed the last drops of water from the rag in his fist. 'I can talk to your mum about it. She could have a word with the principal. Maybe he'd be disciplined by the school.'

'Don't. It might make things worse. He's a dickhead, but I don't want him to lose his job because of me.'

Nathan sighed and dunked the rag again. 'So we just keep on scrubbing, eh?'

'If he keeps on doing it, I'll report it,' I said, but I wasn't really sure if I meant it or not. 'And I'll keep an eye on him at school.'

I'm not sure if Nathan believed me either. We finished cleaning in silence and went inside for breakfast with only the ghost of the graffiti hovering outside our house. Mum had made a special effort to make everything nice. There was orange juice, tea and coffee, fresh cinnamon rolls and crispy bacon, and Saturday morning TV chirruping in the background.

'There's my two working men,' Mum said just a little too

brightly, rubbing my stubbly scalp and kissing Nathan on the tip of his nose.

'Smells delish, love.'

We pretended not to notice that Jamie was only picking at her food, and even though we all saved her the last cinnamon roll, she left the table early.

'Thanks, Mum. Not hungry, though,' she said, pulling her hood over her head. She slouched off to the sofa and disappeared into her phone.

Chelsea came over to hang out, like she usually did on Saturday mornings.

'I told my parents you were helping me study,' she said, as we got some Coke from the fridge. 'They're convinced I'm going to fail everything, never go to college and live in their house forever.'

'I can lend you some notes,' I said. 'What do you need the most? Maths? I'm pretty sure the cosine of pi squared is not a thing.'

'Only you,' Chelsea said, 'would still have their Leaving Cert notes from last year. Nerd.'

'You're far too relaxed about your future – you know that, right?'

'Whatever,' Chelsea said. I followed her to the stairs. Mum and Dad were watching TV on the sofa together. 'Some things are more important than exams. Like figuring out who you are and being happy.'

'And you,' I said, 'are a lazy bum.'

'Fair.'

We'd always sat beside each other in primary school, but when I went to the boys' school and she went to the girls' school, we still made time to hang out together, going to the same shops, or studying at her kitchen table while her mum made us tea and toast, or playing video games in my bedroom. She was the first person I'd said 'I'm gay' to, out loud, and she'd hugged me and told me she'd always known. There was a time when everyone thought we must be dating, even though some people knew I was gay. When they found out we weren't a couple, the rumours started that Chelsea was gay too. She thought the rumours were funny. If girls called her a dyke, she just said, 'You wish!' and carried on being her awesome self. Something weird happened in Transition Year, though. I skipped ahead, and everyone else did their work experience and stuff, but Chelsea just kind of disappeared for a while. She didn't even tell *me* what was up, and we told each other everything.

There'd been all the usual gossip – Chelsea was pregnant, she'd tried to kill herself, she was bulimic – but when she'd come back, turning up in my bedroom one Saturday morning as if nothing had happened, all she'd said was, 'I don't want to talk about it,' and I'd said, 'Cool,' and we'd left it at that. Every so often I'd say, 'You know, if you ever want to talk …' and she'd punch me on the arm and change the subject. But it was nice having her back, even if she did have secrets, so I never brought it up any more.

We went to my bedroom. Chelsea smoked out the window, criticising everything from my taste in music to my taste in men. 'Do we have to listen to this whiny little pop tart again?'

'Aw, come on, don't get ash on my bedsheets.'

'Please. I could probably get pregnant just from sitting on them. Were you wanking all morning?'

'Not all morning …'

'You're gross.'

'I bet you secretly want my babies.'

'If I was pregnant with your baby, I'd take up smoking crack.'

My phone beeped. I dived for it before Chelsea could read the text from Peter.

Hey mate. Had a good time last nite. Fancy a pint next week?

'Yes!' I punched the air.

'That closet case is going to break your heart,' Chelsea said, dropping her cigarette butt into my can of Coke.

'At least he can't get pregnant.'

'You're more likely to get pregnant than him,' Chelsea said, so I picked last night's boxers off the floor and threw them at her. I thought she'd shriek or squeal, but she just sniffed them, made a face and dangled them out the window.

'I'm gonna feed them to Killer!'

'Chelsea! They cost, like, thirty quid!'

'For a pair of boxers? Gays are crazy.'

'Crazy to be friends with you, you panty-sniffing monster.'

We played video games while I played it cool with Peter. I didn't reply for a whole hour.

Love to, mate. It's a date.

Then Chelsea had to go to her part-time job in the book-shop. 'When I dropped out of Transition Year, everyone said I was missing out because work experience was fun. They lied. At least I'll have a job if I fail my exams, though. Later.'

She left. I waved goodbye from my bedroom window, then found Jamie curled up in her room. She stuffed her phone under her pillow as I walked in.

'Hey,' I said, thinking about how quiet she'd been at break-fast. 'Everything OK?'

Jamie sniffed. 'Yeah. But I saw the graffiti on the wall. Who did that?'

'Aaron McAnally. It's nothing. He set fire to my hair in Biology class once.'

That earned a snort.

'Want me to kick his arse for you?' Jamie said.

'Maybe next time. Why don't we go watch crap TV and eat jellies?'

'I'm not hungry.'

'Well, let me know when you are.'

I ruffled Jamie's afro and got up to leave.

She jumped up and gave me a hug.

'Don't worry,' she said, 'most people aren't like him.'

And everything, for now, was OK.

SHED

I know gays are supposed to have the fashion gene, but it must've skipped me. When Soda started sneaking me and Chelsea into PantiBar, we thought we'd be overwhelmed by glamour, but it was just an ordinary pub with a bit more sparkle and a few drag queens thrown in for free. Soda was in his element, Chelsea was, as usual, mistaken for a lesbian, and I was relieved to find out I'm not the only gay in town who can't coordinate an outfit without a whole lot of help.

'Look,' Soda had squealed. 'Double denim! And that guy's tucked in his shirt, but he's got a beer belly. See, Ben? You're not that bad after all. Witness the tragic haircuts, the dad shoes paired with sportswear, the flabby upper arms falling out of tank tops.' Soda paused to check his reflection in the mirror behind the bar before delivering his final devastating blow. 'All the gays are normal now,' he said, 'and that means some of us look like crap.'

I let Soda dress me the first few times we went out, but I felt a bit silly – 'Ooh, the detail on that belt! Have you thought about updating your phone cover to match your shoes? Wear your collar up, it's more rugger bugger' – and I slowly began to piece together what passes for what Soda calls 'a look'. I normally stick to a uniform of skinny jeans, smart polo shirts and colourful trainers, but as I pulled everything out of my wardrobe to find something cute to wear for my second date with Peter, everything I would've once thrown on and thought, 'Ah grand, that'll do,' now looked tired, scruffy and hideous.

Mum poked her head around the bedroom door as I was sniffing the armpits of a shirt I wasn't sure I'd washed since the last time I'd worn it.

'Mum! I'm not dressed!'

'Sure, weren't you born without a stitch of clothing on? I just wanted to say good luck with this Peter fella later on.'

In my mind, I said, 'Thanks for the support Mum, but I'm standing here in my boxers right now. Argh!' But what actually came out was 'Stop jinxing it!'

Mum just ignored me. 'Now don't forget to text me if you're staying at his,' she said, as if I hadn't spoken, 'and remember to bring protection.'

'Mum! I'm not – we're not – oh God, just let me put some clothes on. Please.'

'I just want you to be careful, that's all. I know what people your age are up to.'

'I'm not up to anything. I'm supposed to be going for a drink in half an hour, and I'm still half naked.'

'Make sure you use plenty of lubrication.'

'Mum!'

'OK, OK, I'm going, enjoy your evening.'

I threw on the first clean clothes I could find and raced out the door, pure scarlet, before Mum could demonstrate how to roll a johnny onto a banana.

Chelsea rang as I was heading into town, which was good, because it took my mind off how nervous I felt.

'You'll never believe what happened at work yesterday.'

'Another kid peed in the kids' section?'

'Guess again.'

'That cute bloke who works in deliveries finally asked you for my number?'

'Get real.'

'I give up. Tell me.'

'We had a bunch of little gurriers in – they looked about twelve – and they sneaked right down to the back of the shop and started flicking through the gay erotica.'

'You're kidding?' I don't know what was more shocking – the fact that kids were looking at gay erotica or the fact that I hadn't even known about gay erotica when I was younger. It was probably for the best. I never would've got any homework done.

'Nope. *Look at this! There's two men, and they got all nude, and now they're kissing!* They started reading bits of the dirty books to each other, and we were all standing there not knowing which way to look – I mean, were they actually gay? Like, all of them? – when one of them started acting out the juicier scenes with his mate.'

'You. Are. Joking?'

'No, deadly serious.'

'So what did you do?'

'I just thought, well, sod this, they're too young to be looking at erotica, even if they are gay, which I doubt. There was this old guy leafing through *Giovanni's Room*, and he was mortified. Like, the kids weren't actually customers. I mean, they looked like they couldn't afford socks. So anyway, I marched over, and said, "Right, you lot, you're too young to be looking at those books – they're for adults. Out!"'

'And did they go?'

'Nope. They started calling me a big fat lesbian, and then they knocked a pile of books off a table and threw the collector's edition of *Tom of Finland* at my head.'

'Is that the one with all the big mickeys in it? Ouch. Are you OK?'

'I've got a black eye.'

'You know what that means. Compensation money. I hope the bookshop forks out for the injury and trauma you suffered for just doing your job.'

'You should be one of those lawyers on TV with a fake tan and a shiny suit, telling people to call now on a no-win-no-fee basis because they slipped off a footstool in 1996.'

'Are you really OK, though?' We were laughing about it, but Chelsea got almost as much abuse as I did at school. We'd learned to look out for each other.

'I'm grand. The boss let me go home early. But now I don't know whether I was homophobic for throwing the kids out of the shop, or they were sexist for calling me a big fat lesbian, or whether I should get a nice safe job in a fireworks factory or something. I could mess around with gunpowder and try not to blow myself up. It's probably less dangerous than working in a bookshop. And meanwhile, you seem to think working with kids is fun?'

'What I've learned is kids'll say anything. Don't listen to them. You're not that fat.'

'Wow,' Chelsea said, flicking a lighter and taking a deep drag on the other end of the phone, 'you really know how to cheer a person up. So, what are you up to?'

'Meeting Peter for date number two.'

'Are you going to an actual gay bar this time?'

'Yeah. I suggested PantiBar. Maybe I'll get a snog this time.'

'Hope he doesn't choke to death on a stray sequin. Enjoy!' she said, and clicked off.

I waited outside the pub for Peter. I looked at my reflection in the window, as punters inside sipped their pints, the lazy Sunday vibe broken up by the glittery disco music pouring out into the street. I fixed my collar and ran a hand over my head, glad that keeping it shaved means I don't have to worry about my hair. I saw Peter reflected in the window and turned around to say hello. I was going for a quick man hug, but he stopped short, and I let my arms fall to my sides.

'Why are you wearing that?' Peter said, poking me in the chest.

'What?' I said.

I was wearing the same thing I always wear – jeans, trainers and a polo shirt.

'I'm not sure I like that shirt, mate. What are you trying to say?'

'What are you on about?'

'It's pink. You're wearing a pink shirt. Your top is bright pink, Ben, and we're in public.'

This wasn't how I imagined our second date would start off. I'd been excited to see him all day, and the first thing out of his mouth was he didn't like my pink shirt? I thought we'd have a beer, and maybe he'd slide an arm around me as he gradually relaxed. But no – he was already upset because my clothes weren't manly enough. Maybe I should've worn overalls and a tool-belt. When I'd suggested we meet in PantiBar, I thought it'd be good for Peter to hang out around other gay people. Instead, he kept looking over his shoulder, as if he was paranoid that someone from his other life, his straight life, might see him there.

'It's just a shirt,' I said. 'Anyway, you know what they say. The clothes come off!'

That sounded slutty. Oops. Peter looked at me as if I just didn't get it, shook his head and dived through the door. I wasn't sure if he was really thirsty or just embarrassed to be seen with me in the street. It was probably my fault for dragging him out of his comfort zone. I took a deep breath and followed him inside. A red neon sign lit up the wall, flashing with a pair of cartoon boobs. The nearest window was full of free condoms, gay magazines, and leaflets from loads of different charities, promoting diversity, tolerance and safer sex. I saw Peter turn pale beneath the glow of the flashing neon sign, and tried to see the bar through his eyes.

I thought the lazy Sunday vibe – with special offers written in chalk and everyone lounging around – was welcoming, but how did he feel?

Inside, the disco soundtrack blared through speakers hooked up to one of the bar staff's iPods. The silver mirror ball revolved slowly over an empty dance floor. The guys on their own glanced up from their drinks, looked us up and down, and went back to flicking through their free magazines, which were chock-full of images of tanned, buff, smiling gay men. The crowd didn't match the magazines, and that wasn't such a bad thing. There was an old man in leather trousers sitting on his own, an ageing twink surrounded by shopping bags scrolling through Grindr on his phone, and a smattering of people around our age, in twos and threes, giggling over cocktails. Peter hesitated, clearly torn between dashing back for the door or going up to the bar.

'What are you drinking?' I said, striding over to one of the muscled, tattooed Brazilian barmen, who looked up from polishing a pint glass to flash a friendly smile.

'I might not buy you one back,' Peter said.

'Hey, if you're broke, it's fine. It's on me.'

'I mean, we might not stay.'

'Well, let's see what happens. Pint?'

Peter nodded, peering suspiciously down the row of taps, as if some of the beers might be gayer than others.

'Why don't you find a table, and I'll bring the drinks over?'

This was going to be hard work, but damn it, he was so

handsome. His hair was tousled from nervously running his fingers through it, his scruffy stubble was heavier and sexier than the other night, and I couldn't help imagining how it would feel if he pressed his lips to mine. I watched him look around for a table while trying not to look anyone in the eye. He chose a seat with his back to the window. The light played around his ruffled hair like a halo. I ordered two pints of craft beer. Even though I didn't want a pint, I thought Peter might be annoyed if I got myself a girly drink.

'Don't look around,' Peter said, as I carefully put our pints down on beer mats, 'but that old gay over there has the backside cut out of his leather trousers.'

'They're leather chaps.'

'They're disgusting,' Peter said, which was a bit judgemental.

'He's happy, so who cares?'

'Me. I don't want to look at his old, wrinkly arse hanging out, do I?'

'So don't look at it, then,' I said, trying desperately to think of something to say to change the conversation. 'Hey, I like this song.'

'But he's begging us to look at it, isn't he? He's walking around with his arse hanging out, just begging someone to bend him over and –'

'If you don't like his arse, stop talking about it so much,' I

45

said quickly. 'And anyway, people can wear whatever they want, can't they?'

Peter frowned and took a sip of his pint. He put it back down on the table, but not on the beer mat. Froth spilled over the polished wood. I resisted the urge to wipe it up with a napkin. Instead, I tapped my foot to the music. 'Good tune, though, isn't it?'

'Isn't it one of those *X-Factor* rejects?'

'No, it's that girl band, the one from the hairspray ad.'

Peter curled a lip. I stopped tapping my foot.

'It's all the same shit, though, isn't it? I have this theory,' Peter said, leaning in to explain it to me, 'that all gay guys are deaf. Either that, or they've got female brains. It's like their ears are tuned to a higher frequency than normal lads'. That's why they don't like proper music with guitars and squeal ten decibels higher than they're meant to.'

He leaned back again, satisfied that his theory made sense. As if on cue, the two lads at the table beside us squealed and clapped their hands in unison as the chorus of the song kicked in. Peter grimaced and shot them a dirty look.

'I mean, why do they have to do that? You don't do that. That's what I like about you.'

I knew that was supposed to be a compliment, but it didn't feel like one. I felt like saying, leave the guys alone, they're enjoying themselves, but I didn't want to ruin the mood. Me and my mates got excited about stupid pop songs sometimes. So what?

'What's the big deal?' I said, more sharply than I meant to. 'I suppose you think it's better when men yell at the TV during rugby matches, or grab each other's arses when they score a goal, or punch each other in the face when they get in a row?'

'Well, it's more masculine, isn't it? Those guys look like seals in a zoo, clapping for fish. Come on, you feel the same. Admit it. Why else would you like me? I'm not a typical gay, am I? I'm just an ordinary lad who happens to like other lads too.'

Peter grinned disarmingly, and all the blood in my brain rushed to my boxers. I sipped my pint and looked away.

A couple of tables over, two lesbians, one with a face full of piercings and one in a pink cardigan, kissed. The old man in leather trousers watched a younger queen sashay up the length of the bar. A man dressed as a lady teetered close by us in enormous heels, then paused theatrically with a finger poised to her painted lips and chose a seat at the bar, crossing her legs and pouting over the cocktail menu.

'Don't even start me on drag queens,' Peter said. 'If you're a man who likes men, why would you want to look like a woman?'

'She's a transvestite,' I hissed, 'it's different.'

'Trannies, drag queens, whatever. You can never tell which

of them have got the chop and which are just doing it because they like the feel of silky knickers. It's confusing. You wouldn't know what to expect if you went for a grope – know what I mean?' He must've been able to tell from my face that I wasn't impressed. 'Jesus, I'm joking. Lighten up. I didn't think you'd be one of those boring politically correct types.'

I decided it wasn't the right moment to invite Peter to Soda's drag show.

'So,' I said, racking my brains for the least gay thing I could think of, just to change the subject, 'you never told me what part of the North you're from?'

'One of the scary places on the border, you know? There aren't any jobs there, so I moved. Plus everyone is kind of crazy religious, so it's hard to be gay. I got sick of my family asking awkward questions about why I haven't got a girlfriend yet.'

'Well, I'm glad you moved. I love the Northern accent.'

'Accents,' Peter corrected me. 'We don't all sound the same.' He downed half his pint in one gulp and leaned back.

Oops. I knew that people could be touchy about the Protestant and Catholic divide up North. Had I said something offensive? 'Sure, I didn't mean –'

'So, yeah,' he went on, as if I hadn't spoken, 'Dublin is a shithole, isn't it? If it's not those kiddy-fiddling priests, it's the bankers robbing the ordinary workers. Rent is a joke, and everything is so expensive. But every other city in Ireland is just a bog in the middle of nowhere. So that's why I'm here.'

'Do you miss your family?'

'Nah. They're all saying Hail Marys for me, in case I become corrupted by the gays and atheists.'

'I hope you do.'

'Me too,' he said with a wink, and I relaxed a little – or at least, I would have if he hadn't kept skulling his beer. I thought he was drinking quickly because he was nervous, so I tried my best to put him at ease. We chit-chatted about nothing much, and Peter seemed to relax once he got over the shock of being in an actual gay bar. I couldn't understand why it bothered him so much, but if his family were mad Catholics, that might explain it. And if I didn't understand, then it wasn't up to me to judge his life, right? So I toned down my impulse to sing along to the catchy choruses on the barman's iPod, refrained from commenting on the perils of wearing a size-twelve high heel with a floral kaftan, and agreed with Peter on the ill manners of using dating apps in a bar, but not so loud that the guy on his own scrolling through Grindr could hear us. The lads in the corner were singing with enough gusto to put any *X-Factor* reject to shame, the tall transvestite was feeling beautiful in her big blonde wig, and the ageing twink was extending his shopping trip via the power of modern technology, and good luck to all of them.

The smiling barman came over to wipe down the table top, flashing his teeth and muscles as he mopped up the spillage. 'Can I get you another drink?'

'Sure,' I said.

'No,' Peter said. 'We were just leaving.'

The barman hesitated, looking back and forth between us.

'I guess we're leaving,' I said, with a forced smile.

'Enjoy your day,' the barman said, flashing more teeth and muscles, and swept up the pint glasses.

'I hadn't finished that, mate,' Peter said.

'Ah, my apologies, sir.'

The barman waited politely as Peter took the last half-inch of his beer back, drained the dregs and made a production out of handing the empty glass back to the barman.

'Come on,' Peter said loudly, as if he'd scored some points over the barman, 'let's get out of this kip.'

My face burned in embarrassment as we left the bar.

Peter breathed a deep sigh of relief as we stood outside, the chalkboards, the neon, the torn fly posters around us looking tatty and ghostlike in the pale afternoon.

'Come on,' he said. 'I know somewhere better to go.'

I followed him down a side street and he stopped outside

an apartment block. Gutters spat brown water, graffiti dripped with sleazy slogans, and no one was around. I looked over my shoulder nervously. I could still hear the thump of disco music from PantiBar, but it seemed a world away from the safety of the main street.

'I used to live in this building,' Peter said. Then he slammed me up against the wall and kissed me hard on the mouth. I felt myself resist, then gave in, kissing him back as his hands moved from my chest, to my waist, to my belt.

'What are you doing?'

He fell to his knees, and grabbed me between the legs. I looked down at him and his cheeky grin, scared that someone might come by.

'Stop it,' I said, pushing his hands away.

He groped the hard-on in my jeans. 'I think you like it,' he said, grabbing for my belt.

OK, I was flattered he wanted to, but not when people might be looking. 'Quit that, we're in public!'

Peter jumped to his feet as the front door of the apartment block opened.

A woman with a pram emerged from the doorway, which Peter held open for her, slipping inside as she trundled off with her baby.

'Come on,' he said.

Unsure if what I was doing was smart, but a little bit excited in spite of myself, I followed him inside the apartment block. What was the worst that could happen?

'I lived here when I first moved to Dublin,' he said, pressing a button that released the catch on the inner glass door into the body of the apartment block itself. 'I don't have keys, but you don't need keys to get into the courtyard.'

'I don't think we should be here,' I said, slowly following him through the hall, feeling like some sort of criminal.

'That's what makes it so exciting,' he said.

Further down the hall, he pushed another button that released the door into a small courtyard, propping it open with half a brick that was lying on the ground. 'You need a key fob to get back indoors if you don't leave the door open, yeah?' As I followed him into the courtyard, I wondered if the brick was a lucky find or if he knew it would be there.

He grabbed me by the wrist, and I felt the hairs on my arm stand on end as he led me to a small shed in the courtyard.

The windows of the apartment blocks loomed all around us. No one seemed to be looking. The courtyard was small, closed in, but with plenty of shelter thanks to all the trees and shrubs, which lent some privacy to the space behind the shed.

Peter pressed me up against the brick wall behind the shed and kissed me full and hard. My hands roamed up his back, which was strong and muscular and slightly damp beneath my fingertips, and I felt his stubble scratch my face as I breathed in the scent of his body, the shampoo he used, the musky hint beneath his deodorant.

He reached for his belt and began to unbuckle it.

'What are you doing?'

'Your turn,' he said. 'Get on your knees.'

I pushed him off me. A kiss outdoors was sexy, but anything else felt dirty. 'Dude. That's nasty. I'm not doing that in some random courtyard.' I wiped my mouth with the back of my hand, noticing for the first time all the litter on the ground – crushed tin cans, empty wraps of foil, used condoms, discarded needles.

'OK,' Peter said, his belt dangling open. 'I guess I got the wrong idea.'

'Can we just get another drink?' I said.

'Oh, for fuck's sake.'

'Seriously, though. I think you're hot and everything, but I don't really want to –'

'Don't be such a bitch.'

'Am I more of a bitch if I blow you or don't blow you?'

'What's your problem? I didn't buy you a beer?'

'Huh?' The fact that he hadn't bought me a beer was so far from my mind, it took me a second to focus on what was actually happening. On the fact that we were in someone else's courtyard, and it was daytime, and none of this was sexy any more. 'I don't want you to take your clothes off behind some filthy shed.'

Peter slowly unbuttoned his jeans and began to slide a hand inside his underwear. 'Come on. You telling me you don't want this?'

Maybe part of me did, but Peter wasn't thinking about me. None of this was about what I wanted. 'Not like this, Peter.'

I stood with my back to the wall, feeling trapped, as Peter slowly began to work his hand up and down, and I tried to keep my eyes on his face, feeling a weird mixture of excitement and shame.

04

HOMEWORK CLUB

Monday was kicking my arse.

After Peter had worked himself up into a frenzy behind the shed, he'd punched me on the shoulder, grinned, and we'd gone our separate ways. He'd walked off zipping up his fly, leaving me feeling kind of dirty, even though I'd firmly kept my boxers on. I wondered if there was something wrong with me – wasn't this the sort of sexy, dangerous thing my mum was sure every other guy my age was up to? – and tried to push it to the back of my mind. Maybe I'd have a chat with Soda about it next time he was dragged up. He's easier to talk to when he's a girl. Back home, I'd turned off my phone, gone to bed early and watched Disney DVDs in bed until I fell asleep. Next day, I hit the snooze button on my alarm about ten times, pulling the pillow over my head, refusing to admit that I had to get up and go to work. By the time I dragged myself to the bathroom, I had to brush my teeth and pee in the shower to save time.

I watched it all swirl down the plughole like lemonade with an ice-cream float. Pretty classy, right? I mean, who wouldn't want me as a boyfriend?

Five minutes later, I pulled on my hoodie and legged it out the door, my trainers half falling off because I'd tucked the laces in instead of tying them. I didn't want to be late for signing in at the secretary's office, even though the secretary was my mum.

My day started when the rest of the class went home and the girls in Homework Club stayed behind for extra lessons. I was doing my work experience with seven-year-olds who were struggling to keep up with the rest of the class, giving them extra help with maths and English, and trying to get them used to having a routine. Sometimes I was just happy if they ate lunch with their mouths closed. They were shy at first about having a guy in the classroom – all the other staff were women, apart from Aaron, who was always in the garden – but once they got used to me, we settled into a pattern that worked.

The one piece of advice Mum had given me was, 'Don't be too out, if you know what I mean. Of course you should be yourself, but it's still a Catholic school.'

'So?' I'd said, naively.

'So,' Mum said, 'I can't really talk about being divorced, and you shouldn't talk about being gay. There are still some weird laws about who can be employed in Catholic schools. Just be careful about what you say.'

Luckily, it hadn't been an issue. The headmistress, Miss Murgatroyd, was a born-again vegetarian who wore floaty floral dresses with sandals and smiled at absolutely everything. She didn't mind if I arrived out of breath and a few minutes late, but if I wasn't on time, my mum would shoot me the glare of doom, which made me feel about seven years old again. Luckily the school wasn't far from our estate, so I usually made it on time.

I dashed past the charity shops with depressing bits of china in the window and hard-faced mannequins in second-hand clothes who always seemed to be judging me, because at least their outfits were coordinated. Past the grocer's, where boxes of fruit and veg sat in untidy heaps on outside stalls whether it was rainy or sunny. Past the butcher's, where rows of meat were on display like glittering jewels. I wondered if the way we packaged ourselves on Grindr and Tinder was a bit like the butcher's window, all polished meat and prime cuts, but I was probably just in a weird mood because I'd wanted to text Peter all night, but didn't, because I wasn't sure what to say. I had a feeling that something like: *I really like you, but shouldn't we sort of work up to outdoors sex?* or *Kissing you is awesome, but do you mind if I keep my boxers on?* wasn't the sort of text that was likely to keep him interested in me, so I'd said nothing. It was up to Peter to make the next move. I quickened my pace and wondered if Miss Murgatroyd threw up in her mouth a little every time she walked past the butcher's.

The school was in the same grounds as our local church, which was the scariest building I'd ever seen when I was a kid. It was a girls' school, which had seemed a bit weird to me and Chelsea when we were younger. It still seemed a bit weird now, even though we'd gone to single-sex secondary schools, but what did I know? Apparently girls did better at school when they were separated from boys. It had a massive statue of Jesus with his arms stretched out, rocking a beard before beards became cool. There were two tall trees either side of the entrance gate, one green and healthy, one dead and stalky. I turned the corner, past the beds of flowers decorated with seashells from a school trip to the beach, and there were the mums and dads waiting to pick up their younger kids from the junior classes. They were on their phones or talking in pairs, in tracksuits or jeans, pushing prams or sitting in their cars.

My mum opened the doors, and my working day began.

Everyone knows my mum.

'Howaya, Marie? I got the form for the little one's ADHD ...'

My mum is short and thin and gets her hair done once a week, so it's always bouncy and blonde, even though her natural colour is mousy brown. She wears nice make-up, but not too much. She goes easy on the eyeshadow because these days, the wrinkles don't go away when she stops smiling.

'You slept in, didn't you?' she hissed.

I signed the visitor's roster for temporary staff and shrugged. Mum gets real stressed about work, but I try not to argue about it with her. The ADHD mum kept yakking on so I was able to escape. Mum always takes her work home with her. It feels like she's always sitting in an armchair surrounded by manila folders, legs tucked underneath her, sighing, a cup of tea perched on the arm of her chair, flicking through the endless paperwork. She broke her left arm when she was little, but it wasn't set right by the doctor, so it's not as good as it should be. I still paint the nails on her right hand for her. It's just a part of her, like the way one ear sticks out a little more than the other so she never cuts her hair too short, or how she wears clip-on earrings that went out of fashion in the 1980s but somehow still suit her.

I know I'm lucky because my mum and my stepdad are in love, and that's not something everyone can say about their parents. Some of the kids in the school have horrible lives at home. Still, even though things are good between her and Nathan, it was a big deal for my mum to divorce my real dad at the time. Despite the fact that my dad was useless and Jamie's dad had a good job in the civil service, my granny and granddad didn't approve of divorce.

I remember being in their house on the farm in the countryside when Mum broke the news. I was eight. I had a knot in my tummy and was keeping my head down because the grown-ups were arguing.

'I won't have it,' Granddad had said. 'There's never been a divorce in this family.'

Granny had fussed over the butter dish and milk jug, nervously smoothing down the good lace tablecloth that she only used when the visitors came, even if the visitors were just me, Mum and Jamie. Luckily, Jamie was glued to the TV and too young to understand what was going on.

'You've met Nathan, Dad,' Mum had said wearily. 'He's nice and we love each other. If everything goes according to plan, we'll be getting married after the divorce comes through.'

Granny had put a hand on Granddad's fist as he threatened to slam it through the plate of ham, salad and potatoes. I pushed my food around on my plate, but somehow, I wasn't hungry, even though Granny had made apple tart for dessert. Granddad was mad.

'It's a sin, that's what it is, a sin!' Granddad said, his hands gripping the edge of the table. 'You might get a divorce, but that doesn't change things in the eyes of God. You'll have a husband running around, out of his mind on drink, a lassie born outside of marriage and a poor little lad being raised by a black man. A black man! What will people say about that?'

'He's Jamie's dad,' Mum said, 'and he loves Ben like he's his own son.'

I could feel the redness creeping from my neck up, then draining to white from my scalp down, my body poured full of shame and confusion as Granddad spat all over Granny's dinner. I didn't know what was so bad about Nathan being a black man, I just knew Granddad didn't like it. My real dad being a drunk was the shameful part. It was something me and Mum whispered about at home and never mentioned to the neighbours, not something you could yell about over dinner. I tried to make myself small enough to shrink underneath the table, but it didn't work.

'Marie is right,' Granny had said.

Granddad had just looked at her, dumbstruck. Granny didn't usually contradict her husband, but this time she was determined to speak her mind.

Granny had taken her hand away from his and stuck out her chin. 'Better a man who loves her, whatever colour he is. And isn't it better for both the children to have a father with a job, who loves their mother? Never you mind what the neighbours will say because it's none of their business, and that's the end of it now.' Granny had turned to me as I squirmed in my chair. 'Will you take a biscuit and a cup of tea, pet? All this grown-up talk has you looking fierce pale.'

Still true to Granny's cure-all after all these years, I helped myself to a quick cup of tea and a biscuit from the canteen, picked up the kids' second lunches – they were paid for by the school and left in the canteen – then waited in the corridor for the parents to collect their kids from the classrooms. There's something weird about being back in primary school when you're a teenager. Seeing it as a grown-up makes it seem smaller. The kids' worlds were their homes, their school, and their friends, and the rest of the world was just one big place where things were always different.

The kids filed out, excited to see their folks, chattering about their day's work.

I went inside to where the kids in Homework Club were waiting.

Miss Murgatroyd beamed at me. Jessica almost floored me with a hug. 'Hello, Ben! Guess what we did today.'

I pretended to think hard. 'Spellings?'

'No! It was better than spellings.'

I pretended to think even harder. 'Maths?'

'No! Maths are worse than spellings.'

And then, because Jessica was bursting to tell me the big news, I stopped pretending to guess. You have to play along, even when the kids know you're only pretending. 'I give up. What did you do?'

'We had dance class and Anna forgot her shoes and had to dance in her bare feet but she didn't mind and Roxie fell down on her bum.'

'I fell down on my bottom, actually,' said Roxie. 'Bum is rude.'

'Oh dear. I hope that didn't hurt.'

'I'm a dog!' said Noreen. 'Woof woof!'

Then Noreen crawled around the floor on all fours and tried to bite Anna on the ankles.

Miss Murgatroyd rapped the desk with a ruler, Noreen turned back into a girl again, and they filed out to use the bathroom before Homework Club began.

There were four girls in Homework Club, and they were all there for different reasons. Jessica's dad was dead, and although her mum did her best, she was a bit what Mum would call 'simple', so Jessica didn't get much help at home. Noreen was bright but her mum's boyfriend was in prison, and her best friend was her pet dog. Anna's family were first-generation Romanian immigrants, and they didn't speak English, so there was very little help outside the classroom. Roxie was very bright and very difficult. She copied Noreen's homework when she thought I wasn't looking, teased Jessica for being slow, competed with Anna for being the prettiest, and lived in fear of disappointing her mum.

'Have you noticed that Jessica is getting very clingy with you?' Miss Murgatroyd said. 'I think it must be because there's no father figure at home.'

I hadn't thought about that before. 'I know what you mean,' I said, thinking about how she always hugged me when I walked in the door. 'Is that bad?'

'Just something to keep an eye on,' Miss Murgatroyd said. 'Well, here they are. Good luck.'

The girls came back, excited and chattering. Miss Murgatroyd sighed and opened a plastic container of salad.

'OK, girls,' I said, doing my best impression of a cheerful adult. 'Maths first. And when we've all finished our maths, we'll take a break for lunch.'

'Lunch!' said Jessica, her eyes lighting up behind her pink plastic glasses. The only thing that motivated Jessica to pick up a pencil was knowing she could polish off a packet of cheese and crackers afterwards.

Roxie volunteered to get the plastic box of number cubes for counting. I helped Anna pare her pencil. I praised the neatness of Noreen's handwriting. After the other girls had settled down and began to do their sums, I reminded Jessica that staring into space and twirling her hair wasn't going to help her finish her homework.

'I want to do it with you, at the desk, Ben.'

'OK, come up to the desk and we'll make a start.'

Sometimes the girls vied for attention. The others didn't like it if they thought one girl was getting more.

'It's not fair!'

'Why does Jessica get the most help?'

'I want to work at the desk, Ben, too!'

No textbook on earth could teach you how to deal with this sort of rivalry. I took a deep breath and tried to be sensible, even though I was making it up as I went along. Would Miss Murgatroyd notice if I was out of my depth? 'Well, we can't all work at the desk at the same time. There's only room for two. So once I've helped Jessica, how about you come up to me one at a time and I'll check your homework? Then if you need extra help, we can do it together.'

'I suppose that's fair,' Roxie said airily. 'I mean, Jessica always needs the *most* help.'

I shot her a look, but Roxie's face was the picture of innocence. Miss Murgatroyd was extracting a tricky chickpea from her back tooth and didn't seem to have noticed anything wrong.

Jessica took three trips back and forth to the desk to gather all the number cubes she needed for the first sum.

'It doesn't really matter what colour the number cubes are, Jessica.'

'They have to be red or pink,' Jessica said firmly.

When everything was going well, Homework Club had a nice rhythm, kids counting, pencils scratching, mistakes erased, with the posters on the wall explaining that Dublin is in Ireland, Ireland is in Europe, Europe is on Earth, Earth is in the Solar System, and the Solar System is in the Universe. I wondered if outside in the grounds Aaron was laughing to himself about how he'd pushed me over. It didn't help that Mum was nearby. Mum was always busy with doctors' notes, school fees, paperwork for the girls with special needs, cleaning rosters, recycling drives and keeping all the staff happy. I knew I could rely on her if I needed to. The thing was, I wasn't a kid any more, and I wanted to take care of my problems by myself – especially my problems with Aaron. In a weird way, we were both still at school, and he was still bullying me.

'Twelve!' said Jessica, and my phone buzzed.

'Well done, now write it down,' I said, pulling my phone out of my pocket.

'Jessica's only finished the first one,' Noreen whispered to the others.

It was a message from Peter.

'Do you think you can do the next question on your own, Jessica?'

'No! I need to do it here at the desk.'

'OK, so how many cubes do you need for this one?'

'Um ... Twenty-one.'

'And you have eighteen already. So how many more do you need to get?'

I opened the message as Jessica counted on her fingers across the desk.

It was a dick pic.

An actual, up-close-and-personal pic of Peter's freshly shaved bits.

I almost yelped and dropped the phone. OK, it's not as if I'm unfamiliar with the male anatomy, but come on. I'd already seen more than I'd wanted to last time we'd met.

There was a time and place, and work was most definitely not it.

I quickly closed the message.

'Three?'

'Very good.'

'I'm going to get three pink cubes!'

'Great ...'

I turned my phone off. Jessica went to get the cubes, taking the longest way around the classroom on purpose to delay doing her homework. Miss Murgatroyd had finished her lunch and was correcting papers. I was lucky no one else had seen Peter's pic – I'd probably get fired or put on a register for sex offenders for looking at nude pictures in a primary school – but it wasn't the kind of luck I wanted to press twice. I felt a cold sweat break out on my body as I slipped my phone back into my pocket, feeling like some sort of criminal. Outside, a class of older girls filled up the playground for after-school sports, and life went on.

'Ben,' Anna said out of nowhere, 'are you married?'

'Don't be silly,' Noreen said scornfully, 'he's not a proper grown-up yet.'

'He's probably married, aren't you, Ben?' Anna said, leaping up out of her chair and twirling around. 'He's probably married and has a little baby!'

Noreen burst into giggles as Anna mimicked rocking an imaginary baby in her arms. Jessica looked at them both and put her head to one side.

'I hope Ben isn't married,' Jessica said.

'Jessica loves Ben!' Roxie yelled.

'Now, now, Roxie,' Miss Murgatroyd murmured.

'Don't worry, Jessica,' Roxie said, turning to Jessica and patting her on the arm. 'I'm sure Ben isn't married. But maybe, when you're a grown-up, Ben will marry you then. I mean, you *might* turn out to be good-looking.'

Noreen and Anna covered their faces and laughed.

Jessica looked confused.

'Kids can't marry grown-ups,' Jessica said.

'That's right, Jessica,' I said. 'So all this talk is a bit silly, isn't it? Now, who's got their maths homework finished already?'

'I don't want to do maths. I want cheese and crackers!'

'You know the rules, Jessica. No lunch until we've finished our homework ...'

The class of older girls outside were playing rounders. Aaron was mooching around on the edge of the playground, digging up stray weeds with a trowel. My stomach did that automatic backflip that happened every time I caught a glimpse of my old bully, no matter how many times I told myself I was over it, but now was not a good time to dwell on it. I turned back to the classroom, telling myself to concentrate on my job. The other kids were getting restless waiting for Jessica to hurry up and finish her homework so they could all eat lunch, but there was never any hurrying Jessica. She pushed her glasses up her nose, quietly counting her pink and red number cubes, writing down her answers slowly and carefully. She might've been slower, but it was more important to get them right than to be quick, so I didn't mind if we all had to wait.

I wondered if Peter was annoyed that I hadn't replied to his message.

Finally, after what seemed like ages but was only about ten minutes, Jessica finished her maths homework, and I allowed her to hand out the lunches as a reward. As I reminded them to say please and thank you and not to throw their food across the table, I idly looked out the window. One of the girls lost control of her bat and sent it flying into the shrubbery near our window. Aaron saw it land with a thud and jogged over to where it had fallen. He picked it up, but instead of handing it straight to the girl who'd lost it, he turned to face me, swung the bat in his fists and pointed it at me with a smirk. His back was to the teacher, who was just crossing the yard. It only took a second, but as I stood there, with just the window between us, Aaron slapped the baseball bat into the palm of his hand, mouthed 'You're dead' and turned back to the playground. He handed the bat over to the teacher as if nothing had happened.

I was shaking. Should I run out into the yard, explain to the teacher what he'd done? Would she even believe me? I'd told Nathan I'd report Aaron if he threatened me again – but no. Maybe I was wrong, but it would've felt like telling tales. Besides, there was no proof this time, and I was supposed to be dealing with Aaron by myself. The teacher patted Aaron on the shoulder, he went back to work, and I didn't know what to do.

'Ben! We've finished lunch!'

'Can we play?'

I looked at the clock.

Homework Club was already behind schedule because I'd postponed lunch until Jessica had caught up.

'We still have to do our spellings ...'

The kids groaned, and Miss Murgatroyd smiled at me sympathetically, but there was still homework to finish, and that's why I was here. I would think about Aaron later. I couldn't think straight, anyway. I was completely distracted by the thought of Peter's dick pic, weighing heavily in my pocket.

05

DRAG

Gay bars are different at night. It's as if they're in drag during daylight hours, wearing their drabbest gear in case they scare the locals on their way to the office or the shops, but as soon as the sun has gone to sleep and the moon appears in the evening sky, the sequins begin to shimmer. The mirror ball throws glitter through your hair. The leather gleams on sleek, plump cushions. The neon spritzes into life, casting a flattering filter across every face that floats by, and even the darkest corners of the dingiest bars look kind of nice.

Drag works both ways. Usually, you're ordinary on the outside, and you use drag to express your inner diva, like a superhero doing a quick change in an alleyway. The costume reveals the true nature of your identity, telling the whole world there's something special underneath your spandex. OK, so drag queens don't have superpowers, but they do cheer up a party, dressed up to the nines in clothes their sisters wouldn't be seen dead in, and slathered in enough make-up to put a clown to shame. I have this theory that most people use drag the other way. They dress down to pretend they're ordinary. But it's nice to step out of the ordinary sometimes.

So there we were, a couple of days later, having a few drinks in PantiBar and talking rubbish.

'The one thing I don't want to talk about,' Chelsea said, 'is the Leaving Cert. Anything but exams, please. I'm here to pretend they aren't happening.'

'That bad?' I said sympathetically. 'If you need any more notes, just ask.'

'Someone,' Chelsea said, 'please change the subject. Quick.'

'Good,' Soda said. 'Talking about the Leaving Cert gives me horrible flashbacks. Looking Asian and speaking Irish was too much for some people's tiny minds.'

'At this point,' Chelsea said, 'I'm happy to listen to Soda talk about himself all night.'

'Good, because I've got some things to say,' Soda continued, rifling through Chelsea's bag. 'I'm sick to death of Default Guy. I mean, I went to the cinema today – on my own because you two were being boring –'

'I was working,' I said, 'and Chelsea had an exam that might determine her entire future. Sorry,' I added, as Chelsea almost choked on her beer. I mean, Soda loves giving out to us when we don't act like the supporting characters in his own personal soap opera. You can't let him away with it. 'It's what people do when they're trying to pass as adults in a modern society. How else are we going to get jobs and settle down and get married and adopt kids and become so normal we're invisible?'

Chelsea burped loudly.

Soda put down Chelsea's bag. 'When did you get so political? I swear, ever since the marriage referendum, everyone thinks they ought to be Minister for Gay. Anyway, shut up. I went to the cinema today, eating my feelings in overpriced confectionary, and every single film was about some boring middle-class white guy with boring middle-class white-guy problems.' Soda paused for dramatic effect, sipping his cocktail with his pinky finger raised. 'Even the action flicks were about Default Guy trying to kill the baddies and get his girlfriend back. When did everyone agree to care about Default Guy? No wonder everything is so mediocre. We're all pretending that straight white male angst is the universal experience, but that's OK, because as long as he's able-bodied and educated, he can beat the system, man. You want political? Get me a film about a Gaysian drag queen who's going onstage in five minutes flat and can't find her bloody eyeliner. Chelsea, do you actually own any make-up? Even some black goth lipstick would do right now.'

'Have you ever seen me in make-up?'

'No, but sometimes I fantasise about contouring your cheekbones. You know, a little bit of make-up doesn't hurt. Even just a smidge to cover up your black eye. You mightn't get mistaken for a dyke half as much. Even this,' Soda said, waving Chelsea's leather messenger bag around, 'is less a handbag and more a man-bag. I want to take you shopping. I'm a cliché. I don't even care.'

'There is precisely no make-up in my bag. There never has been. I'm going to the bathroom, and, thanks to nature, I'll have to queue for a cubicle instead of being able to pee standing up. With any luck, I'll miss you lip-syncing to Taylor Swift. Break a leg. And if you can't break a leg, break your neck.'

Chelsea stomped off in a huff, almost knocking over our table with her ample bosom.

'She knows how to make an exit,' Soda said enviously. 'She's a loss to the stage.'

We were sitting close to the bar, where a lipstick lesbian was Instagramming what looked like a designer gin and tonic, complete with berries and foliage.

'My kind of gal,' Soda said, hopping off his seat. 'I bet she can lend me some eyeliner.'

As Soda went to cadge some make-up, I looked around the bar, seeing who'd come along for the show, and vaguely checking out the talent. There were rugby gays, bears and androgynous women with blue manga hair. There were office workers in their work clothes, a polished straight couple who looked like they might've read about PantiBar in *The Irish Times*, and gangs of students from their various universities. None of the guys were as handsome as Peter, but I knew he'd hate Soda's drag act, so I hadn't asked him to come out tonight. For some reason, I'd been thinking a lot about normality, and how we spend so much time chasing this one version of reality we're all meant to buy into. Of course, I think it's great that gay couples can get married. There's no good reason why gay couples *shouldn't* get married, especially if it pisses off people like Aaron McAnally. In generations to come, it's going to be embarrassing to admit I was born in a time and place where gay couples weren't allowed to be as ordinary as everyone else. My grandkids will look up at me with big, surprised eyes full of pity and say, 'Tell us what it was like *before* people were cool, Granddad?'

Another part of me looks at marriage and wonders if it's worth all the hassle. My mum was born in a time and place when marriage was for life, and if that hadn't changed, none of us would be happy now. Not so long ago, in another time and place, it would've been illegal for her to marry Nathan. They're in love, and that's what everyone strives for, even if it takes five or ten boyfriends to find the right partner. I look at all the marriages that fail, and think, yeah, there's something pretty romantic about *not* getting hitched. As Nathan said once, after a really boring family trip around carpet shops and DIY stores, 'Love is finding someone to choose bathroom tiles with and not get bored.' Then he kissed my mum as if they hadn't just been arguing over what shade of grey was best for the downstairs loo. It's confusing.

I downed my beer and imagined living in a world where Peter thought drag queens were fun. Now *that* was the kind of world where I'd be happy to get married.

I stood up and waggled my empty beer bottle at Soda as he lined his eyes in the reflection of the mirrors behind the rows and rows of fancy booze. It was his round. He gave me the thumbs-up and thrust his fake boobs across the bar to catch one of the barmen's eyes. He's a shameless flirt. I blush and get tongue-tied when the short, straight, cute barman even looks at me. I have to remind myself that just because they give you alcohol, it doesn't mean they like you – it's literally their job. Sigh.

My phone beeped as I crossed to the bar to help Soda carry the beers – fake nails don't help when you're buying rounds. It was Peter.

I'm drunk LOL! Where are you?

My first instinct was to lie and tell him I was hanging out with Netflix and a jumbo pack of Doritos, but texting someone drunk is the first sign of having feelings. Score. The question was, should I invite Peter or not? He probably wouldn't want to come. He'd probably have a terrible time. He'd probably hate Soda, and Chelsea already hated him, for reasons known only to Chelsea. I typed a reply but wavered over whether to hit Send.

Your favourite place. PantiBar! Haha.

I reached between some bodies to help Soda with the beers, phone in hand. A couple of bears squeezed in between us and one of them jogged my elbow, dropping his pint. It smashed in a rainbow of sparkling splinters, and I hit Send by accident.

The problem was, he turned around and latched onto Soda.

'Oi! Watch where you're going, you stupid queen!' The bear shook his massive paw at Soda, shaking droplets of spilled beer all around us.

Soda poked the bear's belly with a pink talon. 'Who are you calling a stupid queen, you fat mess?'

'That was my beer, you painted trollop! Are you going to get me another one? Or are you too busy tucking your dick up your –?'

'Whoa, calm down,' the other guy said, placing himself between Soda and the rampaging bear in the lumberjack shirt.

'It was an accident. It was probably my fault. I knocked into her, and she knocked into you. Sorry. I'll get us another round.'

'I don't want another round,' the bear said. 'I want an apology from this rude bitch!'

I was about to say he'd jogged my elbow and spilled his own beer, but the guy was so angry I didn't know if that would make it worse.

The calm guy frowned and put a hand on the bear's heaving chest.

The calm guy was chubby and bearded with curly brown hair – more of a cub than a bear, really – and his eyes took in the older, angry bear from top to toe.

'You know what, Michael? I think you've had enough. I'm sorry your beer got spilled, but maybe it's for the best. You're way overreacting.'

Michael's face was red, veins standing out on his forehead like an alien in *Star Trek*. He stared into Soda's impassive face, and Soda stared back, his eyeliner pointed and perfect, his pout camera-ready, the mask of his drag giving nothing away. I looked around nervously. Were people staring? Were the bouncers going to chuck them out? Was Soda going to get a smack in the mouth?

Michael broke the staring competition first, shrugged and cooled down.

'I'm Gary,' the cub said, turning to Soda and offering a gigantic hand. 'Sorry about that. Hope it doesn't ruin your night.'

Soda hesitated, then took the tip of Gary's forefinger in his dainty claw, shaking it unenthusiastically. 'It would take more than that to ruin my night. I mean, imagine if *my* beer got spilled.'

Then Soda sashayed back to our table, poised and untouchable, as Gary laughed, shaking his head and running his enormous hand through his curly hair. Phew. I felt my whole body relax. Michael grunted something that sounded like it was probably rude. I caught Gary's eyes watching Soda's butt, then I quickly followed Soda through the gap in the crowd. Safely back at the table, Soda handed me my beer, Gary watched us clink bottles, and Michael snapped his fingers in Gary's face. I didn't see what happened next because Peter materialised in front of me, like some other alien from *Star Trek*, and I found myself being attacked by a slimy mouthful of tongue.

'You're keen,' I said, wiping my mouth. I washed away the spit with a swig of beer, which was probably less alcoholic than Peter's breath. 'Peter, Soda – Soda, Peter.' They both eyed each other up suspiciously. 'Soda's just been getting into a fight with some bears,' I said, hoping to break the tension.

'Are you a Chinese dish, or is it just the make-up?' Peter said, and for once, Soda was lost for words. He blinked a couple of times as Peter took my beer out of my hand and drank a big mouthful of it. A trumpet blared, smacking Soda in the face.

'That's my cue,' Soda said, recovering his wits enough to down his beer in one go and hop behind the curtain that separated the entertainer from the entertained. Peter put his arm around my shoulder, and I decided that his racist comment was an off-colour joke. Right?

'I'm pissed,' Peter whispered in my ear, 'otherwise I wouldn't be here. You know that, right?'

Right. I took my beer back out of Peter's hand.

When I was a kid, Granny and Granddad used to take me on day trips to churches, or holy wells, or shrines, hoping that some of their religion would rub off, despite our otherwise heathen household. The shrines were always cold, and my knees were always sore from being made to pray outdoors, but if I was lucky, I'd get an ice cream on the way home. These days, I sit in dark rooms full of glittering lights, nursing a beer as a boy in a dress with fake boobs and a terrible wig mimes onstage to the latest pop legend. It's a bit like going to Mass without the boring bits. There's a man in a fancy frock standing up the front, reciting words that have been passed down from a source of infinite wisdom, saying silly things like 'I live for the applause!'

Just like priests and pop stars, drag queens are kind of needy. They channel the spirit of someone bigger and better because they want your attention. The thing is, some guys are scared by a man in a dress because it reminds them that being a man – the way you talk, the clothes you wear, the way you stand – is theatre too, and sometimes they can't handle it. Drag is funny because it makes us see how we all conform to what's normal. I guess when you struggle too hard to conform, looking at someone who breaks all the rules and gets away with it must really hurt your pride. I guess that's why Peter, who was really into the whole masc thing, mimicked barfing into my pint glass as the curtains opened, the DJ struck a button, and Soda's number blared to life.

I nudged Peter's elbow to tell him to stop, but he just grinned, put his arm around me, and kissed me sloppily in the ear. OK, it felt gross, but I forgave him. It was cute and affectionate, in a puppy-dog sort of way.

True to his heritage, Soda was performing a Japanese pop number, squeaky clean and spiky to my ears, one of which was still recovering from being licked out.

'What's his drag name?' Peter hissed in my wet ear.

'Miss Ugg Lee.'

He was dressed as a cross between a geisha girl and a futuristic hooker, in a demonic green kimono with chopsticks in his wig. His dress clashed with his Ugg boots, which, if I'm honest, looked horrible. I felt a surge of pride that I was finally beginning to understand fashion and made a mental note to tell Soda that his outfit needed killer heels, even if it ruined his drag name.

'Jesus. So the boots are on purpose?'

'You get extra gay points for noticing the boots.'

'What?'

'Never mind. Hey, Chelsea! This is Peter. He just turned up!'

'Hi,' Chelsea said, offering her hand. 'Pleased to meet you, at last.'

Peter grasped her hand and winced as she shook it.

I said a little prayer that Peter would say something nice.

'You should arm-wrestle for a living,' Peter said. 'You'd make a fortune. How'd you get the shiner? Boxing truck-drivers?'

Maybe it was my fault. I was kind of out of practice when it came to prayers.

'That's my dream job,' Chelsea said, looking at me as I mouthed an apology, shrinking a little, with Peter's arm still around my shoulders. 'Enjoying the drag show?'

I said another little prayer that Peter would at least say something pleasant.

'Not really,' Peter said. 'I mean, I know he's your friend and everything, but I'd be embarrassed to hang out with him. No offence. It's just, well, look at the state of it.'

Soda, or rather, Miss Ugg Lee, was hand-clapping along to the chorus, as grown men with beer bellies and skinny gays in designer jeans and pretty girls in checked shirts grinned from ear to ear, their ears thankfully less full of slobber than mine. I ran a finger inside to shift the spit, thinking that a smack on the bum would've been more romantic and less intrusive. I resigned myself to the fact that praying was lost on Peter. If it didn't work for his family, it definitely wasn't going to work for me.

'You could at least lie and pretend you like it,' Chelsea said.

'What's the point of that?' Peter said.

'I don't know – good manners?' Chelsea said.

Ouch. Instead of cringing, I tried to change the subject. 'Hey, does anyone need more beer?' I said, throwing mine back in two seconds flat.

'I think it's good manners to say what's on your mind,' Peter said. 'If you don't like it, then tough. It's not my problem.'

'Oh yeah?' Chelsea said with a snarl. 'Then why don't I tell you what's on *my* mind?'

Peter shrugged as Miss Ugg Lee attempted a high kick, somewhat crippled by her chunky boots and tight, clinging dress. Half the audience winced. The other half cheered her on. 'Total shit,' Peter said, jerking a thumb at the stage, but looking Chelsea in the eye.

'So … beer …' I said, but it was far too late. Chelsea and Peter were nose to nose, nostrils flared.

Chelsea poked Peter in the chest with a big fat finger of righteous anger. She screwed up her face. The bruise around her eye looked ripe enough to burst. 'Guys like you get on my nerves. You act all macho, but that's all it is, just an act. You swagger around like you've got the world's biggest dick between your legs, but you're so scared of looking feminine that even being in the same room as a drag queen turns you into some Neanderthal. You know what?' Chelsea said, as Peter shrank back from her angry face. 'Being a man isn't about having the world's biggest dick. And acting like the world's biggest dick doesn't make you a man. It takes balls for Soda to dress up and get on stage. Meanwhile, you're not even out to your parents. Get a grip.'

The J-pop number ended with a bang as Miss Ugg Lee dropped into the splits.

The pub erupted with whoops and hollers and frantic applause.

I stood frozen between Chelsea and Peter, an icy cold bead of sweat trickling down my spine. I wanted to say something to fix this, but the words wouldn't come.

'Whatever,' Peter said, regaining his composure. 'You're more of a man than half the guys in this pub. Why don't you go fuck yourself? No one else here wants to.'

Chelsea's mouth fell open. I expected her to punch him on the nose, but instead, she grabbed her bag.

'Hey – Chelsea – wait!' I put a hand on her arm, but she shoved it away.

She threw her bag over her shoulder, almost flattening the guys at the next table.

'How did I do?' Soda said, bouncing off the stage and into the middle of the drama, oblivious to the tension as the cheers rang out. The DJ was already lining up the next number for the following drag queen. 'Did you see my splits? I forgot the words halfway through, so I just started chewing my wig.'

'Peter here thought you were shit,' Chelsea said. 'Why don't you ask him?' Then she shoved her way through the crowd and disappeared.

'But Peter's opinion is irrelevant,' Soda said, as if Chelsea was still there and Peter wasn't.

'Drama,' Peter said, rolling his eyes. 'Typical dyke. I'm going to the bar. Who wants a beer?'

I tried to call Chelsea, but her phone rang out. I was going to text her, but part of me was angry with her too. Yeah, Peter had been rude, but that was because she'd overreacted to his not liking Soda's act. Just because all my memories of religion belonged firmly in the past, wrapped up with some of the warmer memories of my granny and granddad's house in the countryside, didn't mean that Peter had shaken off the shackles of prayer as easily as I had. So he had a few issues. It was normal. I could slowly help him get his head around gay culture if my friends didn't start a fight every time he curled his lip at a drag act.

'What the hell did he say?' Soda said, as Peter stumbled to the bar.

Before I could reply, I felt a bulky presence press into my back and an arm reach over my shoulder. A huge paw waved itself in Soda's face. 'Dude! I mean, lady! That was awesome. I love your act.'

I looked over my shoulder and into Gary's happy, bearded face.

'That's so sweet,' Soda said, 'but I only accept compliments in alcohol.'

I grabbed Soda's arm and pulled him aside. The music and the lights seemed suddenly oppressive. We stood still in the middle of a crush of bodies. Everyone was straining to see the next act, but all I could think about was Chelsea. I had to shout to make myself heard over the music, and that made the words even worse. 'He told her to go fuck herself, because no one else here wanted to.'

I was hoping Soda would say something flippant, tell me we

were both overreacting, but just this once, he looked properly worried.

'Oh, that's bad. That's very, very bad. No wonder she's upset.'

'I know it was rude, but she'd already done her death-grip on his fingers, then she poked him in the chest, then she called him a closet case, and –' I was trying hard to find an excuse, I know, but Soda was having none of it.

He cut me off patiently and firmly, the way Miss Murgatroyd did if one of the kids was getting hysterical over something silly. 'No, I mean it's bad that he said no one here was interested in her.'

OK, I could be rational about this. 'Because she's sick of people assuming she's a butch lesbian who doesn't make an effort?' I said.

Soda sighed. He shook his head, false eyelashes fluttering, and calmly adjusted his wig. His painted lips were set in a serious line. 'Ben, you can be so obtuse. The reason Chelsea is upset is because it's true – no one here is interested in her. But she's interested in someone. Understand?'

'No. What are you talking about?'

Soda snapped his fingers in my face, his painted nails clacking like birds. 'Wake up, Ben. Chelsea's in love with you. She's been in love with you, like, forever.'

I stared at Soda in stunned silence as Peter pressed a bottle of beer into my hand. I took a long, hard slug, without even tasting it.

'Hey, I got you a beer,' Peter and Gary said in unison, thrusting a bottle in each of Soda's painted claws.

06

THE BIG FIGHT

I followed my best friend into the night. The air was warm and still. The glow of the traffic lights made coloured masks out of the faces of pedestrians. They stood pressed together but alone in their thoughts, waiting for the lights to change. The lights from PantiBar were reflected in the passing windows of cars. The glow from the pub even spilled into the alleyway across the road, where two men and a woman were huddled up together, drinking cans.

You can't go down a single street in city-centre Dublin without seeing an addict of one kind or another. They hang around in doorways or curl up in sleeping-bags, watching the world go by in a stupor, trying to forget their problems. The cops move them on if they hang around for too long in one spot, but mostly, people leave them alone.

'What are you bleedin' lookin' at?'

The traffic lights turned green and I scurried across the road with the other pedestrians, the woman yelling after me in a cracked, high-pitched voice.

'Go back to your gay bar, why don't you, and leave the people alone! Don't be judgin' me.' Maybe they had nothing left to cling to, except their cans and each other, but I hadn't been judging her. It was none of my business.

I scanned the streets for any sign of Chelsea. She would either walk home, to the right along the Quays, or go to our nearest bus stop, to the left towards O'Connell Street. I took a chance on it and walked along the Quays, seagulls circling the River Liffey above the heads of the tourists, the homeless drunks and the couples on their way home from restaurants and cinemas. The couples held hands and stopped every few steps for a smooch, or a selfie, or to point at the seagulls and laugh. One tourist stopped to take a snap of a homeless man passed out on the boardwalk along the river, in a nest of paper coffee cups and plastic bags full of rubbish.

A seagull got in the way of his photo, so the tourist yelled and shook his fist at the bird. He really should've known better. Dublin seagulls don't scare that easily. Instead of flying off, the seagull swept down and snatched the man's phone with its malevolent yellow beak, flew up, up into the air, and, as the tourist hopped up and down in anger, dropped the phone with a squawk. The tourist dived on his belly to catch the phone before it cracked on the pavement, and I walked on, grinning to myself. Seagull 1: Tourist 0.

I leaned over the wall separating the Quays from the boardwalk and dropped a two-euro coin into the coffee cup clutched between the sleeping man's red-raw fingers. Another time, another day, that man could've been my dad.

I looked up and down the Quays, but there was no sign of Chelsea. I tried calling her again, but she didn't answer. I could risk going left or right, but I might miss her altogether. I shoved my phone back in my pocket.

If I was Chelsea, what would I have done?

As I stood there thinking, the faint beer buzz from PantiBar wearing off the longer I stood in the chilly evening air, a black kid came running up to me out of nowhere.

'Hey, man, do you know where the hostel is?'

His tracksuit was filthy, his accent was inner-city Dublin, and his breathing was hard and ragged, like he'd been running down the Quays for ages.

'Which hostel?'

He hesitated and looked me up and down. Some people would be scared if a black kid in a filthy tracksuit came running towards them, but to this kid, it was people like me who were scary.

'The homeless hostel? I forget the name. It's around here somewhere.'

'I don't know it, but I could look it up on my phone?'

He flinched as I pulled my phone from my pocket. Maybe he was scared I was going to punch him or pull a knife. I wondered how he'd ended up here, asking strangers for directions to a building he didn't know the name of, hoping for a bed for the night. But he was in a different story, and I wasn't a part of his life, wherever that life was taking him. I guess everyone has their own story, and Chelsea was part of mine, and this was the part where I had to find her.

He shook his head.

'No, thanks, I got to be there before the curfew.'

And then he ran on past me, down the Quays, before I could even open Google Maps. Think, damn it. OK. Deep breaths.

If Chelsea had decided to walk home, I probably would've been able to see her along the Quays from here. I tried calling her one more time, with no luck. There was nothing for it. I turned around and ran down Bachelor's Walk, towards O'Connell Street. Round here, anonymous office blocks rubbed shoulders with corner shops, apartment blocks hiding behind tall walls of granite and glass. The early houses were open almost all day, and there were always addicts outside, spending their dole money getting drunk. Their faces were sad underneath their baseball caps, and they nervously sucked on cigarettes before going back inside for another jar.

I wondered where my dad was now, but kept running.

Empty buildings, blank windows. Once upon a time, the street would've been alive with people spending money, tripping in and out of taxis, dressed in designer gear, but now it was tired mums out too late pushing prams and dropping receipts for spent phone credit on the ground, teenage dads crushing cans in their fists, and Chinese and Brazilian students, curtains open and lights on, crammed into tiny flats.

On O'Connell Street, everyone was eating McDonald's or Burger King, waving down buses and taxis, or kissing each other. For a second, staring at all the couples made me wish I had a boyfriend to kiss in the street, but I pushed that thought to the back of my mind because my best friend came first.

I found Chelsea smoking at the bus stop, blowing blue smoke rings into the air. She was the only person waiting, and she was sitting on the ground because there weren't any benches. The timetable said it was five minutes to the next bus. Rubbish lay around like a really lame art installation about the state of the nation.

Chelsea didn't look at me as I sat down beside her.

'You can tell a lot about people from the things they throw away,' I said, looking at the rubbish. Chelsea didn't take the bait, so I kept on talking. 'A beer can. A SIM card. A free newspaper. Oh, look, a used pair of jocks. He should've tried to sell those on eBay, instead of chucking them out the window of the 69X.'

That earned a smirk, which Chelsea quickly covered up by taking a drag on her cigarette. I stuck my legs out and banged my trainers together, not sure what to say. But when your best friend has stormed off with good reason, then there's only one thing to say, especially if she's a girl, and the fella you like hasn't made a great impression, and you feel somehow responsible, even if it's only because you stood there watching it all happen and did nothing about it. I took a deep breath.

'Sorry about Peter,' I said. 'He's not really down with the whole gay thing yet.'

'He's a rude prick!' Chelsea yelled, chucking her half-spent cigarette into the gutter, where it bounced, sparked and died, its sad little soul curling upwards in a final gasp of blue smoke.

'Oh, come on,' I said, 'he wasn't that bad. You should apologise too.'

'What are you talking about? What did I do? Did you hear what he said to me?'

'He's drunk. He was trying to be funny. He doesn't understand our sense of humour yet.'

Chelsea clutched her ears and put her head between her

knees. 'I can't believe I'm hearing this,' she said. 'Do you know what you sound like? You're already making excuses for him, and you've only known him for five minutes. He's not even that hot! You're only obsessing over this guy because he's tortured, and his background is so troubled, and blah blah blah. That's your problem, Ben. You're always trying to see the best in people. Sometimes there is no good side. Sometimes guys are just rude and awful, even if you do think they're handsome. You can't help people all the time.'

'I don't do that.'

Chelsea laughed scornfully. 'Yes, you do, Ben. Remember in Fifth Class when Donal Walsh didn't do his homework, and Miss McMahon did the whole more-disappointed-than-angry routine, and you volunteered to stay in over your lunch break to help him with his geography?'

'Yeah, but no one liked him because his uniform smelled, and everyone knew his mum was an alcoholic, and my mum was pretty sure that his dad beat them up. I overheard her talking to social services. I felt sorry for him, that's all. No one else wanted to help him colour in a map of Ireland.'

'So why is that your problem?'

'If I didn't help him, who else was going to? I didn't like break-time anyway. I didn't want to play football.'

'That's not the point. The point is I had to eat lunch on

my own that day, outside on the corner of the girls' yard and the boys' yard, because you were inside helping smelly Donal Walsh pick the right colour crayon for County Donegal.'

'That was, like, a hundred years ago!'

'And you're still doing it!'

A homeless man shuffled past, his white beard stained yellow with nicotine, his clothes some in-between colour from layers and layers of grime. He was bent almost double, eyes darting around. He spied Chelsea's dead cigarette, pounced on it and tucked it behind his ear for later. We sat in silence. The timetable said our bus would be along in three minutes. My phone rang in my pocket, but I ignored it.

'Aren't you going to answer that?'

'It's probably Peter or Soda. I'll go back to the pub after you get the bus home.'

'Fine.'

The homeless man shuffled off, whistling to himself tunelessly. A chattering conga-line of Spanish students snaked by.

'You never see Spanish students on their own, do you? They're all one big happy family, hanging out in groups of fifteen or twenty ...' I was trying to go somewhere funny with that, but it came out as a really depressing thing to say, especially since it was just the two of us sitting there at the bus stop, not looking at each other.

Chelsea folded her arms and leaned back against the pole with the bus timetable on top.

'Remember my cousin Deirdre's wedding last year?' she said.

'Yeah. They tried to make you wear a big puffy meringue dress, and you threatened to burn down the house and never come home again.'

'Yeah. I never told you about the groom's speech, did I?'

'I don't think so,' I said, wondering where Chelsea was going with this.

'I usually skip the speeches at weddings. I always make an excuse to nip out and have a sneaky naggin of whiskey in the loos, but this time, I came back too early and was forced to sit through Deirdre's husband's speech at the end. He told this story about the two of them going to a football match to support his home team.'

'That sounds nice.'

'It wasn't. *I asked her to go, even though I knew it wasn't the sort of thing she liked. I love football, and she hates sport. But fair play to her, she said she'd go, and she got ready with the sandwiches and the flask of tea. It was a freezing cold day, and I knew she wanted to go home, but she stood there on the sidelines with me as I cheered on my home team. Deirdre stood beside me with a big smile on her face even though she hated every minute of it, and I thought, yeah, that's the woman for me.* And Deirdre just sat there, as happy as could be, as if it was the most romantic thing ever!'

'But he was happy she took an interest in his hobbies …'

'Bullshit! Why didn't *he* take an interest in *her* hobbies? He was chuffed with himself because he found a woman to do whatever he wanted, however horrible it made her feel. She even made him tea and sandwiches into the bargain. It was a test. He put himself first and she let him. What I'm saying is, Ben, don't be like my cousin Deirdre.'

My phone rang in my pocket again. I fished it out. It was Peter. I turned my phone off and put it back in my pocket. More angry seagulls circled overhead.

'Remember all the stuff Aaron McAnally did to me at school?' I said.

'Of course I remember.'

'One time, he trapped this enormous spider with the lid of his flask and said he was going to put it down my boxers.'

'And I wrestled the lid out of his hands and clamped it to his mouth so the spider would crawl down his throat.'

'But the spider just crawled over his face because he kept his mouth shut.'

'First time for everything,' Chelsea said, relaxing enough that her elbow touched mine. I felt myself relax a little too. 'Oh, and remember that time we were in the yard, talking about what we were going to wear for Confirmation, and he said your stepdad was going to make you wear a grass skirt with a bone through your nose because that's what his tribe did back in Africa?'

'Oh God. I forgot about that.'

'And I told him your stepdad kept a lion in the back yard, and we'd feed him to the lion if he didn't shut up. Then Mrs Rice gave us a lesson about Africa being a continent, and people having different customs everywhere, and how great the Catholic missionaries were, and all that stuff. But I caught Aaron peering in your back yard with a big stick once or twice after that.'

'The worst time,' I said, 'was when we had that substitute teacher in, the one with the herbal tea and hippie dresses. Remember on the first day she asked a question, and I put my hand up, and she didn't know any names yet, so she said, "Oh yes, dear, the girl with the pretty blonde hair," pointing at me. Everyone thought that was hilarious.'

'God, yeah. That was awful. Aaron brought that up for years afterwards.'

'He was always pretending to twirl his hair and flutter his eyelashes at me, which made me gay, not him. That's probably why I keep my head shaved.'

'Yeah. I understand,' Chelsea said, crossing her arms so her elbow wasn't touching mine any more. 'I got plenty of that too.

Why do you want to wear a suit for your Confirmation, Chelsea? Don't you want to paint your nails with the other girls, Chelsea? Are you sure you're in the right bathroom, Chelsea? Good job I learned how to give a good kick in the shins, or I wouldn't have made it out of there alive.'

'Hey, remember that time when Josie Winters called you a total dyke, and I said her mum was a total dyke because she was a PE teacher. That shut her up. And then two years later, her mum ran off with the lollipop lady.'

'I guess sometimes the clichés are true.'

'And maybe if I wasn't such a helpful idiot, I wouldn't have been friends with you,' I said, punching Chelsea on the arm, like she was just one of the lads.

'Thanks a lot,' Chelsea snapped, jumping up as the bus pulled into view. 'I don't need your help, Ben. I'm not one of your projects.'

'Hey! Wait. I didn't mean it like that,' I said, but Chelsea had already turned her back on me, waving down the bus with her exact change at the ready.

I leapt up off the ground.

The bus heaved to a halt.

'I think we need some time apart, Ben,' Chelsea said, and the words sounded rehearsed, like she'd been practising them at the bus stop just before I'd found her. 'I can't watch you throw yourself away on this Peter person. And I – I need to study for my exams, by myself, OK?'

'So now you care about your exams?' I said. 'Since when?'

'Since now,' Chelsea said. 'I need to be alone for a while. Got it?'

'Ah Jaysus, love,' the driver said, 'would you cut the speeches and get on the bus?'

'What did I do?' I said.

'Nothing,' she said. 'This isn't about you, OK? This is about Chelsea.'

I watched her pay for her ticket and stomp upstairs without looking back.

Somehow, the way she'd said that – 'This is about Chelsea' – made me feel like whatever was up with her, it had been on her mind for a long time.

I hoped Soda was wrong.

I hoped Chelsea wasn't in love with me.

It wouldn't have made sense. She knew I was gay. We were friends *because* I was gay. It was one of the things she liked about me. She didn't expect me to be one of the lads, always droning on about football and birds, and I didn't expect her to be an empty-headed girly-girl, like so many other people did. I liked the way we chugged cans together, and talked about joining the gym but never did, and made stupid plans to go

Interrailing around Europe, or start our own YouTube channel, or skip college to open a pet-grooming business, but then ended up watching DVDs all night, talking about which actors were fit, and which of them had earned their abs at the gym, and which of them had paid some cosmetic surgeon for an enhanced six-pack.

'We should just pay for them,' I'd decide, and then she'd hit me with a pillow.

'Lazy arse,' she'd say. 'Where are you going to get the money from?'

'Maybe I'll sell my lazy arse and make some money. Quit judging me!'

And then we'd fall asleep, me prising the smouldering cigarette from between her fingers, thinking it would be nice to have that kind of banter with another guy. But much as I loved Chelsea, I just didn't love women's bodies like I loved men's, and that was never going to change.

I stood there on O'Connell Street, looking up at the top deck of the bus, hoping that Chelsea would at least wave goodbye to me.

'Ah, would you cheer up,' the bus driver said. 'Sure, a pretty boy like you can do much better than her.'

I didn't know what to say to that, so I just shook my head, and the bus driver sighed, as if all the advice he'd ever given in his life had been ignored.

Having Chelsea on my side had always been like having a straight guy there to protect me from the worst of the insults. She spoke the same language as the playground thugs like Aaron, Darren and Wayne, knowing exactly what to say to shut them up, just like I'd known how to shut up the girls who'd tormented Chelsea when our teachers' backs were turned. It would've been nice to have a boyfriend who stuck up for me that way.

The bus drove off with Chelsea on it. I didn't even see her at the window on the top deck, so she must've sat on the opposite side to avoid looking at me.

Well, now I was on my own – and that made me realise something. If I didn't stand up to Aaron McAnally all by myself in front of his stupid mates, then he'd always be able to bully me, school or no school.

I turned on my phone and rang Peter back. 'Hey? Yeah. Sorry about that, Chelsea was … Yeah. Cool. I'll see you in five minutes.'

Back at the bar, Peter stuck his tongue in my ear instead of saying hello, and I didn't have the heart to tell him it felt a bit gross, because it still felt better than someone else disappearing in a huff.

07

PILLS

I woke up feeling mouldy. I was face down in a puddle of my own drool, naked from the waist up but – I peeked under the covers – yup, still wearing my jeans and trainers. My head was clamouring with the tinny, persistent, anguished souls of one thousand car alarms. I Snapchatted a pic of my hung-over face to Peter, making sure he got a glimpse of my chest too, then hauled myself off to the shower.

Kicking off last night's clothes felt like being reborn, but as the hot water sluiced over my face, the images of the night before played in a loop across my mind.

They weren't pretty.

I remembered Peter being way too drunk and insulting Soda. I remembered Peter trying to put his hands down my boxers at the bar and having to stop him. I remembered thinking I'd give Chelsea time to cool down after she went home, but I'd tried to call her in the taxi on the way back to mine, the beer and the blues and the blur of the traffic making everything seem more urgent. Up until then, the rest of the night had been good, despite the drama. We'd danced to trashy pop, watched the other drag queens perform a Spice Girls megamix, and I'd got leered at by some old bloke in the toilets, but kept on drinking. Bits of the night kept coming back to me in flashes, like stills from a music video caught in the glow of a strobe light, slowed down so that one girl flicking her hair, one lad's laughing mouth, and the crowd accidentally synchronising their dance moves to one perfect pop song all added up to the memory of having fun. But the feeling that something was wrong still lingered. Maybe I'd drunk too much beer. Maybe it was because I went to bed without speaking to Chelsea. Maybe it was because I'd lost Soda towards the end of the night, but then, that always happened.

He was always disappearing off to some guy's house on the promise of free beer and a cuddle. I could've done with a cuddle, to be honest. After all that happened, I'd felt a bit let down by Peter, only reluctantly kissing him goodnight in the bar, even though his version of kissing me goodnight was to try to chew my head from my neck.

I towelled myself dry and checked the mirror for hickeys. I'd have to wear my collar up today to cover the dirty purple bruise floating over my collarbone, ripe and heavy, like a cloud about to rain. I texted Soda, pulled on clean clothes, popped my collar, ran a hand over my head – I'd need a haircut soon, the stubble was starting to grow out – and went downstairs, following the smell of frying bacon.

Mum was making pancakes, flipping them expertly despite her lame arm, which kind of puts me to shame. The only thing I can do with both hands is too rude to mention at the break-fast table.

'Morning, son,' Nathan said, peering over his newspaper. He's so old-fashioned he actually reads newspapers. Even though he has an iPad, he mostly uses it for cheating on the crossword. 'Whoa. Looks like you had a good night.'

'Why's your collar turned up?' Jamie said, as she pushed cereal around her bowl. I wondered if she was actually eating. Nathan and Mum exchanged a look that told me they could guess why my collar wasn't buttoned flat, as usual.

'It's called fashion, Jamie,' I said. 'I'm, like, a totally fashion-able gay person. Um …'

Jamie rolled her eyes, Nathan laughed, and Mum handed me a stack of bacon and pancakes with a kiss on the cheek, pretending not to peer down my collar for clues.

'Hey, they're not the sort of kisses Ben goes out looking for till three in the morning,' Nathan said, and I turned scarlet as him and Mum laughed like hyenas.

'Gross,' Jamie said, pretending to barf into her cereal. Nathan ruffled her afro and Mum sat down for breakfast, smiling to herself, which makes her look ten years younger than she does at work.

Soda texted back as I was smothering everything in maple syrup, and I quickly texted him back to say I'd meet him around the corner after breakfast.

Nathan's eyebrows almost flew off his forehead. 'Is that Mr Loverboy? Don't reply so quickly – he'll think you're too keen.'

'It's only Soda,' I said, secretly annoyed that Peter hadn't Snapchatted me back, even though he'd opened my pic.

Nathan did the washing up, Jamie slumped in front of the TV, and Mum sat down with an armload of paperwork to finish for school. I sneaked off to meet Soda by the recycling bins. It was mostly tarmac with a small patch of grass and a big metal fence. It had become our place to hang out when we were too lazy to go into town. Soda would walk up from Smithfield and we'd take photos of graffiti to put on Instagram and chill.

Soda looked completely different out of drag. He looked boyish, even though you'd never exactly call him masculine, not that he'd care. His hair was longish and floppy, he had a wide, bright smile, and he carried himself differently in jeans and a hoodie – loose-limbed and easy-going, unlike Miss Ugg

Lee, who was all posture and angles. Soda always had his fair share of chasers coming after him in drag, but beneath all the make-up and female body armour, I was sure he wanted someone to like him for the boyish Soda. He waved his hands at me, and I grabbed him by the hoodie, pulling it over his head and wrestling him into a headlock.

'Quit it, if you want your stash in one piece!'

I let him go and he punched me on the arm, lightly, more in protest than in earnest. I grabbed him by the ears and he pushed me away with a grin.

'Save the rough stuff for Peter, you big fool. Do you want the drugs or not?'

'Shush, would you? People will think you're dealing.'

'Well, I am, sort of. This is all highly illegal.'

'Don't be silly. It's poetic justice, and no one's going to get hurt. Do you have them?'

'Twenty euro, please,' Soda said, drawing the white paper bag out of his pocket and dangling it in front of my face.

I took the cash out of my wallet and we solemnly swapped substances for currency, as has been tradition at the recycling bins since forever. It's the local hotspot for buying weed off your neighbour's cousin's boyfriend, or underage drinking on the night of your Junior Cert results, or, rumour has it, getting a wank from Shelley Matthews for a fiver.

'Remind me why we always meet here?' Soda said.

'Force of habit,' I said, peeking in the bag, then shoving it in my pocket.

'The graffiti is always racist and homophobic,' Soda said, tracing the latest epitaphs under his fingernails, which looked weird in daylight because they weren't glued on.

'Yeah,' I said. 'And it's probably Aaron and his scrawny gang who did it. That's why I've got these, isn't it?' I patted my pocket, grinning my face off.

'It's a nice day, though,' Soda said, throwing himself down on the grass. 'The kind that reminds you how halfway across the globe glaciers are melting, sea levels are rising, endangered animals are being driven to extinction, islands are being submerged under tsunamis, and entire cultures are being wiped out thanks to global warming.'

'What's nice about that?' I said, kicking a tin can at Soda.

'Well, look at it this way,' Soda said, catching the can unexpectedly. 'People talk about the luck of the Irish, and I think, really? Have you ever picked up a history book? Colonialism. Famine. War. Religious oppression. Still, when it comes to the carbon emissions, we're doing pretty well. Longer summers, milder winters and less rain and snow. If we're heading towards the end of the world, Ireland is the place to party. Thanks, global warming!'

Soda crushed the can in his fist and chucked it over his shoulder.

'Nice. You're doing your part for global warming,' I said. A fresh breeze kissed the litter around the recycling bins, making crisp packets dance in the overgrown grass.

'The bins are sort of like the lungs of the estate, right?' Soda said, ignoring me. 'And the houses are the brains. The play park is the heart. The roads in and out are the limbs. The bus stop is what we'll politely call the digestive system. The people are the blood. Well, some of them are more like a virus, but you know what I mean.'

'So what are the grassy bits?'

'They're, like, the armpits,' Soda said. 'And the overgrown bits over there by the bus stop are the pubes. And they need a trim. Yuck.'

'Never mind that,' I said. 'Let's get down to business. Do you want to hide by the bus stop and record the whole thing on your phone?'

'I would, but my battery's nearly dead. Think you can capture it?'

'I can try. You better stay out of the way. Killer doesn't know you, so she'd probably go crazy if you came skulking out of the bushes. OK, it's almost time. You ready to do this?'

'Go for it, girl,' Soda said. We bumped fists, flipped our

hoodies up and stalked off towards the McAnallys' house.

Soda mooched over towards the bus stop. A bunch of old grannies were clinging to their tartan shopping trolleys for dear life. They were waiting for the bus to town to do their weekly shop. Collectively, they gave Soda a suspicious look. They probably thought he was a foreigner who didn't speak English, and therefore wasn't to be trusted, but that suited us fine right now. He stood looking through the glass panel at the back of the bus stop, with a clear view of the McAnallys' front garden.

Thanks to Soda, no one was looking at me. Because they had an end-of-terrace house, I could sneak around the side. I kept my head low down behind the bushes, in case any of the family came out the back door. I peered over the top of the hedge that separated the garden from the pavement.

Killer was sunning herself in the grass. I took the white paper bag out of my pocket, took out the box of tablets as quietly as possible, and crouched down by the end of the hedge, where there was a gap.

'Here, girl. Over here. Good girl ...'

Killer came bounding over, yapping. This was the dangerous part. My heart was in my throat. If Aaron came running out of the house brandishing a baseball bat, what would I do? I tickled Killer's ears and let her slobber on my hand, then tipped a handful of cylindrical green tablets into my palm. They looked evil, but Soda's cousin was a vet, so they wouldn't do the dog any harm. Killer gobbled up the tablets without so much as a pause. Now, if I'd timed this just right, Killer would be back in Aaron's arms at just the right moment ...

'Good girl. You're almost as dumb as your owner, aren't you?'

I heard sharp voices raised in the kitchen. I patted Killer's head and ducked behind the bushes again. Killer, however, was not happy to see me go. She leapt through the gap in the hedge just as Aaron appeared in the back yard.

He threw a careless goodbye over his shoulder to his mother. His phone was pressed to his ear. He was just in time to see Killer's butt disappear through the gap. The dog threw herself into my arms, which was awkward, as I was trying to stay crouched down and hidden.

'Killer! Bad girl!' Aaron yelled. 'OK, yeah, I'll see you in a minute,' he said to whoever was on the phone. 'Bye!' He hung up. It was too late for me to make my getaway. I stood up, the dog in my arms, as Aaron's head appeared above the bushes.

'Not you again, you dog-napping fairy! What's your problem? You can't have babies, so you have to steal other peoples' pets? You're sick. Give me back my Killer.'

'I'm so sorry, Aaron. She just came running at me. It's almost as if she can't bear living with your family. What a clever little doggie.'

'Hand her over, or I'll call the cops.'

Aaron punched 999 into his phone, and I quickly thrust the dog over the bushes.

I glanced towards the bus stop, where Soda had his face pressed open-mouthed to the glass. A bus pulled up, and as the grannies were about to get on, Darren and Wayne got off, almost knocking them over. Darren and Wayne were wearing their best tracksuits, which meant they were all heading into town to hang out at Centra, like they did every Saturday. Perfect.

I slipped my phone from my pocket as Aaron smothered Killer's slobbering jowls with kisses. Then I slid open the camera and surreptitiously pressed Record on video mode.

'Hey, Darren, Wayne! The gay boy is obsessed with my dog. I caught him trying to steal her from under my nose.'

'Your poor nose,' Darren said, sauntering over from the bus stop.

'Leave his nose alone,' Wayne said. 'It's never been the same since the boxing match.'

'Hang on,' Darren said, pointing at Killer. 'Is the dog OK?'

Killer was wriggling in Aaron's arms, as if she wanted to get away.

'She's fine!' Aaron snapped. I held my phone up at what I hoped was a discreet angle. None of them noticed. 'She loves me more than that smelly little gay boy. Don't you, girl?' His voice got babyish as he talked to his dog. 'Let's go get cans and a chicken fillet roll and check out the ladies, like normal lads.'

And as Aaron pressed poor Killer up to his face, planting a smacker on the dog's nose, the dog howled, farted and unloaded a spectacular chocolate mudslide all down the front of Aaron's tracksuit top.

Soda howled from the bus stop.

Darren and Wayne howled in disgust.

It took Aaron several seconds to realise what had happened.

He looked at Killer. His nose wrinkled. Then he looked down at his chest, which was flooded with runny, stinking dog mess. His grey zipped top was splattered with brown, icky poo. He yelped, dropped the dog and ran into the house.

'*Woof!*' said Killer and scampered off.

Soda's cousin's dog laxatives had done the trick.

It had gone even better than I'd hoped, and I'd captured the whole thing on my phone. Win!

Darren and Wayne gawped at each other in horror, then, despite themselves, began to laugh, until they collapsed into heaps on the grass.

'Hey,' Darren yelled. 'Mind the wet patch!'

I'd uploaded the whole thing to YouTube in seconds flat.

I did a little victory dance as Killer dragged her butt across the grass.

'Sorry, girl,' I said.

I was sauntering back to Soda, phone in hand, watching the likes rack up on YouTube and feeling pretty chuffed with myself, when I heard a commotion. I raised my head from my phone to see Soda banging on the bus shelter and pointing through the glass to somewhere over my shoulder. I spun around. Aaron was snarling in my face. The world slowed down, like that moment in a film when something big is about to happen, and you know you've got to pay attention.

Aaron raised his fists. He was topless. His teeth were bared. His eyes were shining with rage. His face was red and livid. I didn't have time to think. He swung a punch at me, and I raised my hands in front of my face. I felt his knuckles *thwack* against my phone, which went flying through the air. I heard it clatter, but Aaron already had his face pressed to mine.

'What did you do?' he snarled.

'I didn't do anything. You were already full of shit.'

'You're some smart arse. Who do you think you are? You think you're so much better than us, don't you? With your fancy clothes and your fancy haircuts and your fancy cocktails. Well, I'm a real man. Take this, faggot!'

Aaron drew back his arm to throw the full force of his fist in my face.

I ducked as he swung his arm, pulled up as he staggered

forward, and punched him square on the nose. His hands flew to his face. A stream of blood trickled through his fingers. His eyes brimmed with disbelief. To be fair, I couldn't believe I'd done it, either.

'Go tell your mum a faggot punched you in the face,' I said, and walked off with my head held high. I was floating on a cloud of cool rage.

Soda came running from the bus stop and high-fived me. 'Did you see his top? Did you see his face? Where did you learn to throw a punch? That was awesome!'

'I don't know,' I said. 'I didn't know I had it in me.'

'That was so cool!' Soda said. 'Did I ever tell you about my brush with death? Back when I was dating Casper, the Muslim guy from Kazakhstan?'

I looked over my shoulder. Aaron was already storming indoors, clutching his nose, followed by his barking, farting dog. Darren and Wayne were dumbstruck.

'Once or twice,' I said.

'It all came to an end when we took a holiday in Galway,' Soda said. 'Someone pulled a knife on us on the way home from the pub. I said, run, but Casper stood his ground. It was romantic, but it was stupid, and we had a massive fight about it. I *might* have given him the teensiest slap across the face, but anyway, by the time he went home to Kazakhstan that summer, he was further back in the closet than my winter wardrobe from 2009.'

'That's sad,' I said, although I was only half-listening.

'The end of a decade is always a sad time for fashion. You're tired of your old look, but you're desperately looking for something new. I'll be hobbling around on a Zimmer frame before cut-off cargo pants and spiked heels are back in fashion.'

'I meant about Casper, going back in the closet,' I said automatically, with the part of my brain that was used to listening and reacting to Soda.

'Oh, that. Well, it could've been worse. He could've gone back to not drinking. Last time I saw him, he was having pints with some fat old git. I don't know if it's worse when your ex trades up, or trades down.'

Which was all very interesting, but right now I had other problems.

I found my phone on the ground, but it was smashed to pieces. The screen was so badly cracked that chunks of glass had fallen out like broken teeth. I scooped up its remains and wondered if Peter had sent me a cute selfie before my phone had nosedived into the pavement. I also told myself that, just like Soda's ex, Peter's troubled background of religious mania and cross-border persecution definitely counted as a good reason for staying in the closet, so not to worry too much about it.

'Never mind,' Soda said. 'I'm gonna share that video on Facebook, Twitter, Instagram ...'

I picked up the littlest pieces of glass as Soda spread our victory across social media, wondering if Peter could get me a new phone from his shop for free. I knew he was off work for the next couple of days, but I could go into the shop where he worked after that. I didn't think he'd mind if I asked for a freebie, and if he couldn't do it, I'd be no worse off than now. Besides, it would be a good excuse to see him again.

Meanwhile, I looked at my own fist in disbelief. It still felt weird that I'd punched Aaron in the face. I usually hated violence, but I had to admit, it had felt good.

At the same time, Darren and Wayne were on their way back to the bus stop. They had gone beyond dumb and now looked awestruck. I cradled my broken phone in my hands as they walked past, warily.

'Huh,' said Darren. 'I bet you can't afford a new phone, though.'

'Can I borrow the fare, Darren?' said Wayne. 'I'm broke.'

A bus swung into view as Soda replayed my video on his phone, howling once more at the sight of Killer emptying her bowels across Aaron's tracksuit top.

Darren ran for the bus. 'I just want to say,' Wayne whispered, 'that was pretty cool. I don't care if you guys are gay, OK?'

'Hey, Wayne,' Darren shouted, 'are you getting in or coming out?'

'Getting in,' Wayne shouted, and scurried off.

'Almost gives you hope for humanity, doesn't it?' Soda said. 'Oh, wow. Look at how many likes you're getting on YouTube, girl!'

I looked at the pieces of my broken phone. 'Don't you ever get sick of being the nice guy?' I said.

'I'm a drag queen, honey. I'm not the nice guy. That's you, Ben.'

'Yeah, well. It gets tiring.'

'I bet it does. That's why I'm always horrible to everyone.'

I took a deep breath.

What I wanted to say was, look at the referendum. People went out and voted so that guys like me and Soda could get married. People, straight people, gay people, all sorts of people, went door to door to ask for the right for everyone to marry the person they love, and they did it for us. I wasn't surprised most people thought that was cool. I wasn't surprised most people wanted us to be happy. What I really didn't understand was people like Aaron, who still thought we were less than they were because of who we dreamed about getting married to one day.

But I couldn't find the words.

'I'm sick of it, Soda,' I said. 'We always have to act better than them, just so we don't get beaten up. I mean, gay people can get married now, right? So why can't all the sore losers just leave us alone?'

'We should get married and piss off the racists too,' Soda said, kissing me on the nose.

'Ah, shut up. You'd only outshine me in your big fancy wedding dress.'

'Come on,' Soda said, throwing an arm around my shoulders. 'I know how to cheer you up. Let's go tell Chelsea about Killer's little accident.'

But Chelsea wasn't answering her phone or her door.

08

VIOLENT GIRLS

'How did people live without smartphones?' I moaned.

Mum had nipped home on her tea break to pick up some paperwork, and I was feeling sorry for myself because my phone was broken. How was I supposed to know if Chelsea had updated her Snapchat story since the night she'd stormed off? It was Monday afternoon, and I hadn't seen her since last Wednesday. I hoped she really was studying and not avoiding me. Meanwhile, I couldn't even keep track of how many likes and shares my video had got on YouTube.

'We used phone boxes,' Mum said, plonking her handbag down and sinking into her favourite armchair. 'Sometimes you had to queue outside a phone box with a pocket full of change you'd saved all week, dancing about on tiptoes in the cold, waiting for whoever was ahead of you to stop talking. Stick the kettle on, I've time for a cuppa before I go back to work.'

'But didn't you have phones in your houses?'

'If you lived in a rented flat, you mightn't have a land-line. Or it could have been in the hall, and you'd have to share it with all the neighbours.'

'But say you were meeting someone for coffee, and they were running late. Like, how did you let them know?'

'You didn't. You might've made the date a week before. Let's meet at Clery's clock at 3 p.m. next Wednesday. Then you'd have to remember, and hope your friend remembered, and hope neither of you was running late.' Mum ran a hand through her hair, as if remembering the stress of it all still made her flustered.

I filled the kettle, shaking my head in disbelief. 'But so many things could go wrong.'

'You waited for fifteen minutes. If your friend didn't turn up, you made other plans. Sometimes you'd wait for half an hour, if you were sure your friend was coming. There could've been a bus strike, or maybe they ran into someone they hadn't seen in years, or the landlord called in …'

'Imagine standing around for half an hour without a phone to play with,' I said, feeling sorry for people in the past. 'No wonder people read books back then.'

'People still read books!' Mum said. 'Don't tell me I've raised a philistine. And anyway, we would've had a Walkman with us too.'

'Yeah, with *one album* at a time,' I said, as the kettle began to bubble. 'On *tape*. Living in the past must have sucked.'

'I suppose it did,' Mum said, 'but we didn't know it then, so we didn't really mind. Everyone was rich on TV, but everyone was poor in Dublin. The height of sophistication was going off to Spain for a week in the summer, and now, that's as cheap as getting the train to Belfast. We were worried about other things, like whether workers' rights were going down the toilet, or if student grants were enough to live on if you were poor, or whether you'd get a better job if you moved to London.'

'Some things haven't changed then.'

'We should think of things to do with disused phone boxes,' Mum said. 'Something useful for the community.'

The kettle clicked off.

'Superhero changing room, that's a classic,' I said.

'There aren't any superheroes in Dublin.'

'I suppose not. Oh, I know,' I said, filling the teapot. 'Karaoke booth. Sometimes you just have to sing out loud.'

'No one deserves to have to hear you sing. You're a lovely boy, but you always were tone deaf. Such a shame,' Mum said wistfully. 'I could've put you on *The X-Factor* and made a fortune.'

'Ugh, no thanks. Hey. What about turning them into showers for joggers?'

'They're transparent!' Mum shrieked. 'Who'd want to watch people showering? I've raised a pervert, as well as a tone-deaf philistine. Oh well, at least you make a good cuppa.'

'Didn't perverts used to put up ads in phone boxes?'

'Sure it's all online now, isn't it?' Mum said vaguely. 'Although I suppose you still get crazy people putting posters on lampposts, and scrawling dirty things on bathroom walls, and writing in to the newspaper with daft ideas.'

'Even if we did recycle phone boxes,' I said, pouring out the tea, 'people would still use them for shooting up, or getting pregnant, or urinals.'

'You see it all in Dublin,' Mum said. 'Now, where did I put my notes?'

After tea, I went with Mum to the school. Aaron was cutting the grass. He scowled at me as we walked past, but said nothing. I don't think Mum noticed.

Jessica threw her arms around my knees as I walked in the door. 'Hey, Ben! What's for lunch today?'

'Hey, Jessica. I don't know what lunch is yet, but I might let you hand it out later, if you're good.'

'Yay!' Jessica said, hugging my knees.

'Guess what?' I said. 'Hugs don't work on me.'

Jessica looked up at me with big, surprised eyes, magnified by her glasses. 'They don't?'

'Nope. Guess what does work on me?'

Jessica scratched her head. 'Coffee?'

'Oh,' said Noreen, 'I make coffee for my ma and my da when they're in bed together. He's not my real da, but I call him my da. I'm allowed to use the kettle and everything.'

I'd been warned that Noreen's mum's boyfriend had been recently released from prison, but Noreen seemed happy about it.

'That's a good guess, but it's not coffee.'

'Sweets!' said Anna, racing over to the bag full of lunches. 'Do we have sweets for lunch?'

'Don't be silly, Anna, you know you don't get sweets for lunch.'

'I know what works on Ben,' Roxie said. 'Homework!'

'That's right, Roxie. Well done. If you all do your homework nice and quickly, we'll have lunch. And if you all finish your homework and tidy up after lunch, then you can all play.'

'Yay!'

'But everybody has to finish their homework and tidy up, OK?'

'Come on, Jessica,' Roxie said, dragging Jessica off my legs, 'that means even *you*.'

I sat apart from the kids for a change, to see if they could get organised by themselves. Roxie found Jessica's missing maths copy, Noreen loaned Anna her second-best pencil, Jessica shared her pink and red number cubes with everybody, and everything was going fine. I only had to coax Anna out from under the table once, convince Roxie that she wasn't going to bleed to death because she'd bitten her fingernail close to the skin, remind Jessica that she was allowed to hand out lunches if she kept up with the rest of the girls, and ask Noreen four times not to share her answers.

The girls worked steadily while I sat back, glad that Aaron would have to leave me alone from now on. My prank video had probably been seen by everyone in our estate. By the time I got a new phone, I'd have dozens of messages of congratulations to look forward to. Peter might even be inspired to come out to his parents knowing you could stand up for yourself and win. Chelsea would come over, give me a high-five and everything would go back to normal.

Anna looked up from her homework. 'Jamie Edwards is your sister, isn't she?'

'That's right.'

'Is your name Ben Edwards?'

'No, I'm Ben Brennan.'

'Like Mrs Brennan in the office?'

'She's my mum.'

The kids were all listening now.

'But that means she's Jamie's mum!' said Jessica.

'Everyone knows that, Jessica,' Roxie said. 'Ben, don't mind what Jessica says. She's *slow*.'

'Why are you not black?' said Anna.

'They have different dads,' Noreen said, rolling her eyes. 'Isn't that right, Ben?'

'Yeah, that's right. My dad was white but Jamie's dad is black, and that's why we have different surnames.'

'Me and my new baby sister *or brother* have different dads too,' Roxie said.

'All families are different,' I said. 'Now, are we ready for lunch? Don't forget to say please and thank you, and no mixing up your yoghurt and your milk to make a milkshake this time. It always makes a big mess.'

'I hope it's going to be a baby girl,' Roxie said. 'Boys are smelly, burping and farting all the time.'

'Roxie, don't be rude,' I said.

'You know what I'm talking about, don't you, Ben? You're probably farting right now!'

The kids collapsed in giggling heaps as Roxie ran around screaming 'I'm a smelly boy!' and blowing raspberries in their ears as Jessica handed out the lunches. That was the end of getting any work done. Sometimes, when the principal wasn't present, the girls got giddy. It was time to bring out the threat.

'Do you want me to get Miss Murgatroyd?'

'She can't stop me,' Roxie yelled, stabbing Noreen with her plastic spoon. 'I can do whatever I want!'

'Roxie. Desk. *Now.*'

I didn't raise my voice, but I did try to sound firm. The girls fell silent as Roxie trailed her feet all the way up to the desk, her eyes on the floor.

'It's OK to have a laugh, Roxie, but it's not OK to use rude language in class. I don't want to have to tell Miss Murgatroyd that you're being naughty, so I need you to be on your best behaviour for the rest of the day. Why don't we have lunch, and then play quietly until home time, and I won't have to have words with your teacher – all right?'

'I'm sorry,' Roxie said, in the baby voice she uses when she doesn't mean it.

'OK, good girl. You can go back to your table now, as long as you behave yourself.'

'Do you want to hear a funny story?' Roxie said, lifting her eyes from the floor and smiling a big smile.

'Yeah, yeah, yeah!' said Anna.

'The butcher said he was going to chop up my dog,' said Noreen.

'Funny stories make milk come out my nose,' said Jessica.

'I was in my estate, right?' Roxie said. 'And there was this gay boy who wanted to play with all the girls, and I said you can't play with us, you're a faggot, and punched him on the nose, and there was blood everywhere, so there was!'

Anna's hand flew to her mouth.

'Uh oh,' said Noreen.

'Ben, can I have some more crackers?' said Jessica.

'Hang on a second, Jessica. Roxie, first of all, I hope you didn't punch anyone,' I said. I was uncomfortably aware that I'd punched someone on the nose that weekend, but I told myself that was different. 'That's not funny. It's really, really bad to hit other people, so I hope that was a joke. But even if that was a joke, we can't have language like that in the classroom. I have to talk to your teacher about that, I'm afraid.'

'What language?' said Roxie in her baby voice, which meant she knew exactly what bad word she'd used.

'I'm not going to talk about it, Roxie,' I said, trying to hold my temper in. 'Sit down and finish your lunch. Miss Murgatroyd will speak to you later, OK?'

It was one thing to hear it from Aaron, but it was another thing to hear it from Roxie. No matter how much things improved, there was always some other kid getting punched in the face and called a faggot, and it still made me angry every single time.

'You're in trouble,' Noreen said, as Roxie sat down and peeled the lid off her yoghurt. 'You can't say that to Ben, because …' She trailed off, looking at me.

'I'm not saying anyone's in trouble,' I said, 'but I expect better manners from you four.'

Outside, I could hear the splutter of the motor from Aaron's lawnmower. I could also hear all the taunts that I'd grown up with, the bad words I'd got used to over time, the chants of boys and girls in the playground who'd known I was gay before I did and never let me forget that it was wrong. Sometimes, even now, years later, the words replayed over and over in my mind.

Roxie was probably too young to really know what she was saying, but you had to tackle it now, before she became the next Aaron.

'Ben? Ben? Can I have more crackers, Ben?'

'Sure, of course you can, Jessica.'

It was almost home time before I was able to catch a frazzled-looking Miss Murgatroyd leaving her office and rushing by the classroom, just as the parents were arriving to pick up their kids. I was nervous about having to explain what had happened. Part of me didn't want Roxie to get in trouble – she was only a kid, after all – but another part of me wanted her to realise that what she'd done was wrong. Either way, it was my job to put my feelings aside and tell Roxie's teacher the facts.

'Miss Murgatroyd? Can I have a word?'

'It's not the most convenient time, Ben,' she said, running a hand through her messed-up hair.

'It's important. It's about something one of the girls said in class.'

I took Miss Murgatroyd aside to a quiet corner of the classroom. She listened to the story in horror as the girls put on their jackets and tidied away that day's homework.

'I'll have to speak to Roxie's mother, but she won't be very happy about it …'

The girls left one by one, except for Roxie and her mum, because Miss Murgatroyd took them into her office. I felt sorry for Miss Murgatroyd for having to deal with it all, and stood looking out the window, gathering my thoughts. Then I stayed a bit longer than usual to tidy up the classroom for the next day. Jessica had left a crushed biscuit on the floor, Noreen had forgotten to pare her pencil into the bin, and Anna had left her maths folder behind. I didn't want to run into Roxie and her mum on the way out, so I hung back, but I could hear raised voices through the wall. Outside, Aaron turned off his lawnmower and stood close by Miss Murgatroyd's office window. Was he listening in? A door slammed, and Roxie's mum dragged her daughter down the corridor. I slipped into the kitchen and left through the back door, hoping to avoid an awkward encounter on the way home.

I walked through the playground, minding my own business, but couldn't help noticing something strange.

Further off, at the edge of the grounds, in the shadow of the statue of Jesus with his outstretched arms and hipster beard, a little gang of three people were huddled up. Two of them were deep in conversation. It was Aaron and Roxie's mum, who looked furious. Roxie was staring at the ground, looking embarrassed.

I turned away and walked home, telling myself not to worry, but not quite able to shake off the feeling that something bad was about to happen.

09

BEAR-HUG

I decided not to talk to Mum about Aaron – not yet, anyway. First of all, I had no idea what he'd been saying to Roxie's mum. Second of all, and not that it makes me proud to admit it, I'd have to own up to the trick I'd played on him, and I didn't want Mum to know I was a YouTube sensation in our postcode area. I decided to sleep on it for a day or two, but at the back of my mind, I was still worried.

Next day, I walked into town to meet Soda. We'd been chatting on Facebook because my phone was still banjaxed, but two days without a phone was as much as I could handle. I was excited by the idea of seeing Peter at work, though. I could imagine him in action with his customer service skills, joking with the lads and flirting with the ladies. I remembered not to wear my pink polo shirt, in case I gave the game away and Peter got embarrassed. So, I wore blue, threw on a hoodie, scrubbed my face and made myself generally presentable to the outside world.

When guys online say they're straight-acting, I always imagine them wearing yesterday's boxers, spraying deodorant on without showering and forgetting to fix their hair. Still, I didn't want to show up in a rainbow flag. I just wanted Peter to treat me like a normal customer, maybe wink at me when his manager wasn't looking and give me a free phone. Was that really so much to ask?

I walked on, daydreaming, past the flats that led into town. Posters advertised gigs, plays and club nights. Some random graffiti urged me to Beat Up Cops. A tourist on a Dublin Bike cycled up the footpath, almost collided with me, then wobbled away shaking his fist, as if it was my fault he was in the wrong place. A young boy in his mother's high heels teetered out on to his front porch, squinting up at me with a serious expression, as if daring me to make fun of him.

I wondered if that was how Soda had started.

'Good for you, kid,' I said.

Further on, a shadow disentangled itself from the gateway of an apartment block across the road, tall, skinny and dressed in what looked like last night's clothes. He rubbed his face as he stepped out into the sun. I guessed he'd crashed in a stranger's bed for the night. We were about the same age. He stumbled across the road in my direction, oblivious to traffic, and swayed slightly before stepping up onto the kerb. He looked like he was still drunk. He was wearing a tracksuit, an eyebrow piercing and a neck tattoo.

He looked me up and down. 'See you,' he said, staring at me, eyebrows drawn together in concentration.

'Yeah?' I said nervously, wiping the sweat from my palms.

'You're a handsome little fella, aren't you?' he said, grinned and walked on.

I'm not going to lie, I was well chuffed.

I looked back over my shoulder to see the tall boy vanishing up a side street by an early house and the young boy teetering back indoors. The tourist on the bike had wobbled out of sight.

Soda was sitting in the window of McDonald's when I got there, stirring his cappuccino, legs crossed, eyebrows raised in disbelief at the catwalk that was the pavement outside.

'This is why I love going to McDonald's for coffee,' he said, as I sat down beside him. 'Apart from the fact that everywhere else is too pricey, you get to see so many people passing by. Look at her eyebrows! Drawn on with a Sharpie. And the tattoos on your man over there. Must've got them in prison. That would explain why he walks funny. Hey, let's turn on Grindr and see if any of the staff are bored out the back.'

'I don't have my phone, dopey. That's why I'm in town, remember?'

'Oh, yeah. Here, look at mine.' Soda's phone buzzed as he turned on Grindr. 'I've got she-mail! Oh, wait. You're not allowed to say that any more.'

Outside, smartly dressed women walked by, tapping on their phones. A couple of lads went past with their hands shoved down their tracksuit bottoms. Shops sparkled with stuff in every window, as flower-sellers yelled up and down the street. People queued patiently outside a bank. A girl checked her hair in the reflection of McDonald's window, her face just inches from mine, and walked away. Pigeons pecked at crumbs on the pavement, and a young guy in a sandwich board advertising a net café shooed them with his foot.

I went to the counter and ordered a coffee from the perky barista. It was the sort of job I could get during college, making coffee, learning how to draw swirly patterns in the foam, trying not to scald my hands on the coffee maker. I tipped the barista because he was cute and wondered if Peter was having a busy day.

Back in the window, Soda was still flicking though profiles.

'Bloody hell,' I said, sipping my coffee. 'How many apps do you have?'

'Dating apps? Well, there's Grindr, Jack'd, Scruff, Man-hunt ...'

Like a business sourcing coffee beans, Soda's approach to flirting is global.

He pointed to a profile. 'So, like, this guy woofed at me all the way from Minnesota. Look at his muscles. He probably eats his own weight in corn-fed chicken every day. And this guy sent me a wink from Sapporo. Nice to know I'm big in Japan. Oh, he looks cute, he's from Melbourne. I like the way his ears stick out. He's a bit too kinky, though. It's hard to make out his face behind that leather mask. Ew.'

'Have you met every bloke in Dublin?'

'Only the cute ones. Don't be jealous. Hey, look, I have my drag profile on this one ...'

At first, I'd been amazed to see so many cross-dressers on Grindr, but according to Soda, it was just one of those rec-reational hobbies that gay guys who are in touch with their feminine side might indulge in.

'There seem to be a lot of Asian cross-dressers, Soda.'

'Good bones, darling. Small noses. We're just prettier.'

There's something cool about being potentially connected to whole tribes of gay people around the world. When you're a kid, and you realise you're gay, you think you're the only one in your neighbourhood. Then you grow up, get the internet and realise there are far more people like you out there than you suspected. At first, it's a bit like discovering you've got super-powers, even if your superpower is just dancing to Lady Gaga in your bedroom, or liking every photo your online crush posts on Instagram, or knowing instinctively which girls won't freak out when you tell them you like boys too. But then you begin to wonder where you fit in. So, you might join the gym and show off your muscles, or take up drag and go to fun parties, or just try to blend in and hope someone realises what a nice guy you are. I was hoping that was my superpower.

'Oh, wow, look at him,' Soda said, thrusting his phone under my nose. 'He's perfect. He looks straight. He's just toned enough. He's got the right amount of facial hair. Not too tall, not too short. Top. Hey, this guy's my new boyfriend. And he's only 783 metres away.'

'What does it say on his profile?'

'Let's see. Oh.' Soda's face fell. '*No fats, no femmes, no Asians,*' he read. '*No offence, it's just not my thing.*'

Gay dating can be horrible.

I took a sip of my coffee, shook my head and stuck my middle finger up to Grindr.

'What a dickhead,' I said. 'You need someone who appreci-ates Miss Ugg Lee.'

'Oh well,' Soda said, putting down his phone and pouring

an extra sugar into his coffee. 'At least I'm not fat, right? And besides, drag chasers are the *worst*. Remember Ronnie, the mechanic from Phibsborough? He was sexy but, girl, he had issues. First, he only wanted to make love when I was in drag. Then, he wanted *me* to make love to *him* when I was in drag. But what really ended it was when he wanted to take me to his sister's wedding, only I had to pretend to be an actual woman. Next!'

Like I said, Soda is a little bit older than I am. When he's not doing drag for kicks, he works as a supervisor in a call-centre for some IT firm – not very glamorous, but it pays the bills. We met online and hit it off – not in a sexy way, just as mates. I needed someone to talk to, and sneak me into gay bars, and give me advice. He needed an audience. And like I also might've mentioned, beneath all the sparkle beat an actual human heart, although Soda did his best to hide it. Sometimes he just wanted to cast his feather boa aside, peel off his fake eyelashes, throw one leg over the arm of the sofa, pour a glass of Aldi's second cheapest white wine, and talk about all the boys who'd broken his heart. He'd told me so much about them, I felt like I'd been there, peeping in through the windows, watching the first kisses, the jealous fights, the passionate making up and the inevitable destruction, which always seemed to have ended with Soda hurling a glass of Aldi's second cheapest white wine in his boyfriend's face, picking up his feather boa and flouncing out with his head held high, but his heart crushed into a cold fistful of glitter.

'Just watch you don't develop diabetes with all that extra sugar.'

'Nervous habit,' Soda said, heaping the sugar into his coffee anyway.

'What have you got to be nervous about?'

'Oh, nothing. A date. I don't know.'

'You've got a date?' Usually, I heard about Soda's dates before they'd even picked a place to meet. 'Why didn't you say so? Who is he? Show me his pics.'

'I don't have any pics.'

'I mean face pics, Soda. Come on. You never meet anyone without at least three face pics. You taught me that. You said everyone has at least one good face pic. So far, so good. Then you ask for a second pic to make sure the first one wasn't a fluke. Then you ask for a third pic, taken right now, to make sure he's the age he says he is, and he doesn't have time to choose a flattering filter, and he hasn't put on twelve stone since pics one and two.'

Soda stared into the depths of his cappuccino, swirling the froth around with the last of the unmelted sugar. 'I didn't meet him online,' he mumbled.

'What?'

Soda lifted his head and stared at me with troubled, pleading eyes. 'I know it's a bit weird, but I met him in real life. Down the pub. I know, I know. Hopelessly old fashioned. Who meets people in real life any more?'

'Hey, I think that's cool. There's something nice about meeting guys the old-fashioned way. So, who is he?'

Soda sank his face into his hands.

'What?' I said. 'Why are you acting so weird?'

'Do you promise not to judge?' Soda said, peeking out from between his fingers.

'You're really scaring me. What's so bad about this guy?'

'I don't know what's wrong with me,' Soda said with a groan. 'I know it's bad, but I like him. I really like him. And he likes me, even though I was rude as hell to him when we met.'

The faintest glimmer of understanding twinkled in my brain, like a stray sequin dropped under the sofa. 'You don't mean Gary?' I said, thinking of the way the young cub had pressed a beer firmly into Soda's hand.

'Oh, Ben!' Soda cried. 'How can I date him? He's – he's – he's *fat*!'

10

MEANWHILE, BACK IN THE CLOSET

'So he's a bit on the large side,' I said. 'So what? You like him, don't you?'

'Yeah, but I'm not supposed to. That's the problem. I'm a skinny bitch. I have a certain image to maintain. My fans expect Miss Ugg Lee to be glamorous, and fabulous, and beautiful, and only date wealthy international supermodels.'

'Uh huh. And how's that working out for Miss Ugg Lee?'

'Pretty terrible,' Soda said, slumping in his chair and looking out the window as cute couples walked past, hand in hand.

'There's your answer. Come on, Soda. Drag is a laugh and everything, but you're just a Dublin queen with a smartphone and a head full of dreams. Miss Ugg Lee is the glamazon you wish you were. This guy sitting in front of me in a hoodie and battered old trainers is far more likeable. Go on a date with Gary and see what happens. No one's judging you. No one cares. Whoever you're dating, bitches are gonna bitch, but when you're wrapped up in your boyfriend's arms at night, they'll be jealous.'

'I can see them now,' Soda said, 'fretting over the calories in their Tesco microwave meals for one. When did you become so wise?'

'I guess listening to you has finally paid off.'

'Oh, I'm always drunk. You should never listen to a word I say, girl.' Soda sucked the last dregs of cappuccino from his cup, but I could tell he was pleased.

'Besides,' I added, 'look at all the guys on Grindr with their *no fats, no femmes, no Asians*. Do you really want to be like them?'

'Hey. I'm not ready to delete Grindr just yet. It's one date, not a marriage proposal. He hasn't even seen me in my boy clothes yet.'

'What's not to like?' I said, punching Soda on the arm.

He punched me back, and I ruffled his hair – 'Watch it. Gay rule number one: don't touch the hair!' – and I left for Peter's phone shop, while he left for his date with Gary.

On the way to the phone shop, I daydreamed about how

things would be when I was in college. Because Chelsea was in her final year and I was taking a year out, it meant we'd be students at the same time. We might go to different colleges – I knew I wanted to be a teacher, and she wanted to study English, although her parents were already worried about her finding a job afterwards – but even so, we could still hang out. I couldn't imagine starting a whole new life, with a new set of friends, and not having Chelsea be a part of it. It was too strange not having spoken to her for almost a week. As soon as I got my new phone from Peter, I'd call her and make it up.

Despite everything, life felt good. Outside an ice-cream shop, I watched a kid try to eat a cone but somehow manage to get it all over her face. Her father wiped it up with a napkin, playfully scolding her. She laughed, then wiped the ice cream all over her face one more time, just so he'd have to clean her up again. It was so cute. I wondered if I'd ever have kids, even though I could barely keep the cactus in my bedroom alive, never mind an entire child. To be fair, I was pretty sure Chelsea used the cactus as an ashtray when I wasn't looking.

Yeah, OK, she could be annoying, but I missed her.

There was a queue in the phone shop. I saw Peter at the counter, but I stood in line like everybody else. I was behind a girl with an enormous red weave and nails so long I was amazed she could still type a text message, a farmer up from the country who kept shaking his ancient brick of a phone in total disbelief that it wouldn't work, and a Brazilian lad whose tight jeans and muscle-top provided a bit of eye candy while I stood there waiting.

If Peter caught my eye, would he call me over? I hoped he'd notice me, but I was partly blocked from view by the enormous red weave, and besides, he was going through a tricky contract with a thin-lipped greyhound of a woman, who looked like she was used to barking orders at people.

There were only three people working in the shop.

The queue moved slowly.

As the greyhound woman left, and the Brazilian replaced her at Peter's counter, Peter cast a look down the queue and did a double-take when he saw me standing at the back. I leaned around the enormous red weave and lifted my hand to wave, but he snapped his eyes back to the counter, and didn't even glance at the muscles straining through the thin fabric of the T-shirt in front of him.

I dropped my hand.

He'd blanked me.

He'd totally blanked me.

He'd totally blanked me, and he was too embarrassed to even check out the hot guy standing in front of him, as his eyes darted from side to side, looking at the customer's phone, looking at the customer's bill, looking at the posters on the wall, looking everywhere, in fact, but at the customer's sculpted torso. I mean, come on. Ignoring the guy you're kissing when he appears at work is one thing, but even I was checking out the Brazilian guy, and I only had eyes for Peter.

And that was when I knew Peter was deeper in the closet than I'd imagined.

The farmer and the girl with the enormous red weave were served in turn by each of Peter's colleagues, leaving me at the top of the queue, waiting for the Brazilian to leave. I could see Peter dragging out the transaction, casting nervous glances at his colleagues, trying to work out how long they would take to serve their customers. He was trying to dodge me. But the Brazilian left promptly as soon as his query was answered, and Peter finally raised his eyes to mine, nodding briskly.

I took my place in front of his desk.

'Hi, I'm Thomas, how can I help you?'

I found myself staring at Peter's name badge, which inexplicably said THOMAS. 'Hi ... Thomas?'

Peter stared back at me. His jaw was tight because he was clamping his mouth shut. He was staring at me intently, as if trying to communicate telepathically, his brain saying something like *Don't make this awkward for me!*

He cleared his throat. 'Yes, it's Thomas,' he said, curtly. 'Now how can I help you today, sir?'

So that was how we were playing it.

'Well, *Thomas*, my phone broke when someone punched me for being gay.'

Peter, or rather, Thomas, winced. 'Is the screen smashed?' he said, pretending not to have heard the part about being gay-bashed. His face was pale and sweaty as he asked all the necessary questions – 'Bill pay, or ready to go?' 'Do you have insurance?' 'Would you prefer a repair or a replacement?' – but I answered robotically, staring at Peter's handsome, scared face and wondering what was so terrifying about me that he had to pretend not to know me at all.

Was I too gay to talk to in public?

Was he afraid I'd make a scene, demand an upgrade, black-mail him into giving me a better deal?

Did he imagine I was going to start calling him Peter, and tell the whole shop how I needed my phone back to talk to closet cases on Grindr?

OK, so a part of me was tempted to do just that. But the bigger part of me, the rational, realistic part, just felt sad – sad that Peter, or rather Thomas, had lied: lied about his name, lied to his colleagues about being straight and lied to himself about having to stay in the closet. My friends had been right. I was cooler than that. I needed someone who was equally cool.

'So, we can offer you an upgraded package deal, with a new handset ready to take away today?'

'Sure. Sounds good.'

'If you just sign here, please, sir.'

Peter's hand – would I ever get used to thinking of him as Thomas? – was trembling as he gave me the pen to sign my new contract. I thought about how excited I'd been when his name had flashed up on my phone, and how it wasn't even his real name. I thought about how handsome he had looked in his Grindr photos, and how my heart had raced when he looked even more handsome in real life. I thought about how there was no going back from finding out you'd been lied to, and took my new phone with a nod, then turned to leave without saying thanks.

'Next,' said Peter – no, Thomas – and I thought, *Yeah. Next.*

I decided to stay off dating apps for a while.

Outside the shop, my head swam. The sunlight hit me like a wall, and I stopped dead in the middle of the street, passers-by looking at me weirdly.

I switched on my new phone, updated the contacts, then found Peter's name – no, damn it, Thomas's fake name – and deleted it. The buildings around me stopped swaying. The lights that spelled out brand names, business logos and *Sale Now On!* resumed their normal place in the world, just a gloss washed over the experience of walking down the street. People stopped looking at me funny, and I straightened my polo shirt, shoved my phone in my pocket, and walked along with the crowd. I'd got as far as McDonald's when my phone buzzed.

Unknown number.

Thomas, of course.

I never lied. Peter is my middle name. I just wanted to keep things separate from my life at home. OK?

But it wasn't OK. Not for me, anyway. Thomas had his own problems, and I hoped he sorted them out for his own sake, but they weren't my problems any more.

I got another takeaway coffee, just for something to do, and enjoyed the small ritual of pouring sugar granules onto the coffee foam, watching them sink with a sigh, each granule bursting with tiny bubbles before breaking through the white froth, dissolving into the depths of the coffee, becoming infinitely small, swirling, helpless.

I don't even like coffee that much. It was just something to do while I tried not to think about Thomas.

I wondered if Chelsea would finally accept an apology.

She'd been entirely right about Peter, and I'd been an idiot. I'd even apologised for him. The memory made me physically cringe, and I clutched my coffee cup too hard, making a little spurt come out the spout and dribble down my thumb. I had to tell Chelsea that I'd been an idiot, and that I should've listened to her the very first night when she'd been at her window and told me Peter was all wrong for me, and that I *really* should've listened the night they'd met and he'd been rude and she'd disappeared in a huff, and how there was no excuse for me putting some dumb guy before our friendship, and I missed her, and I just wanted a chance to make things OK again, if she'd only answer her phone and let me explain.

I tried to put it in a text message, but it came out all long and garbled and it didn't make sense. It wasn't really the sort of thing you could say by text. So I tried to call her, but her number rang out, and I'm terrible at leaving coherent voicemails, so I hung up. Then I tried to reach her on Instagram, cursing the public Wi-Fi for being so slow. After scrolling through my followers, then the people I was following, then typing her name in three times, and even once in Irish, I eventually realised that Chelsea had either blocked me or suspended her Instagram account.

This was serious.

Could she really be that upset over a tiff about a guy?

I texted one of her friends at school to ask if she'd seen Chelsea lately, and if she was OK. She texted back almost straight away.

Saw Chelsea for French exam. She went straight home after. She didn't stick around or talk to anyone.

I began to worry. On the plus side, I was just around the corner from the bookshop where Chelsea had a part-time job, so I decided to go in and see if she was there.

She wasn't.

The manager peered at me through tiny rimless glasses, down the longest nose in the world. 'Chelsea is taking some time out,' he sniffed, 'to focus on her Leaving Cert. Which is, I believe, reasonable.'

'Oh,' I said. 'Do you know when she'll be back?'

'I couldn't say,' the manager said, dangling fingers over an urgently ringing telephone. 'She requested some time off, for reasons of a personal nature, after the exams. But if you see her, do tell her we wish her all the best. Hello?'

I was dismissed from the bookshop, none the wiser as to where Chelsea was.

Irrelevantly, I wondered if the manager's ridiculously long nose made it awkward for kissing.

Outside, I kicked the pavement for no good reason and tried to think what Chelsea might be playing at. If she wasn't talking to her school friends, and she wasn't in work, then she had to be at home, so why wasn't she taking any calls? It was just like the time she'd dropped out of Transition Year and no one had seen her for a few months, except this time Chelsea had disappeared because we'd had a row. It was my fault.

I didn't believe for a second she was worried about her exams. She never had been before. She would do well in English and less well in maths; she would get solid results in French and history, same as she did in her mocks. She'd applied for courses in arts, psychology and media studies, all within her predicted points range, and wasn't too fussed about which course she got accepted for. 'It's college,' she'd said. 'The whole point is to have a good time, not work.'

I began to imagine all sorts of things – she'd run away, she'd had an accident and ended up in hospital – but I knew that was stupid. If either of those things had happened, her parents would've let us know. This was something secret, something that Chelsea didn't want to talk about, and because I'd been a bad friend, she didn't want to see me.

It was turning into the worst day ever.

I wandered up and down the street, trying to think, and sat on the edge of a kerb to calm down and decide what to do.

First things first. I might not be able to reach Chelsea, but I could reply to Thomas.

I get it. It might be OK for you but it's not OK for me. Probably best if we don't see each other. Good luck.

I hesitated before I sent it. It sounded so final. I asked myself if I really wanted to cut all ties, if I could get over his issues, if I could help him through them – but I knew it was no use.

Chelsea had been right. Thomas needed to help himself, and I needed to stop making excuses for him. What had we shared when it came down to it? A good first date, a terrible second date and a bloody awful third date. He had great arms, but a lousy personality. I felt my heart rise as I hit Send, free of the burden of worrying about Thomas's problems.

I got up off the kerb and walked home. I have to admit, I felt a bit sad. All I really wanted was a boyfriend to cuddle with when we woke up hung-over, the kind of guy who'd tell me I looked cute even when we both knew I needed a haircut, someone to eat pizza with when we were both in our boxers. But there was no superpower that let you feel less sad, so I just had to feel it and try to do better next time. I thought about all the good things in my life – my family, my friends, my work experience, the fact I could afford to buy coffee I didn't even like – and felt a bit better. Earphones in, I had a moment when I almost wanted to break out the dance moves in the middle of the street, but I just kept on walking.

Back home, I stood in front of my house, looking from my front door to Chelsea's front door and back again.

Well, she couldn't avoid me forever. She needed to hear that I was sorry, and that, technically, Peter didn't even exist.

There was no sign of life behind Chelsea's bedroom window, so I walked up to her front door and knocked.

Her mum answered. She looked as if she'd been crying, but I pretended not to notice. I felt as awkward as the time I'd come over to apologise for breaking her potted plant with a football.

'Oh, hi, Mrs Nealon. Is Chelsea home? I know she's probably studying, and there are some English notes I said I'd give her, because it's not like I'm ever going to read *Jane Eyre* again. Only I haven't seen her for a while, and I wondered …'

I stopped talking, because Mrs Nealon gave a great big gulp, clutching a handkerchief to her face.

'Is – is everything OK?' I said. 'Has something happened?'

'Everything's fine!' Mrs Nealon said quickly – too quickly. 'Chelsea, um, has to stay away from her friends for a while, Ben. At least until the exams are over. Stress. Anxiety. Doctor's orders.'

Mrs Nealon gave a fake little laugh and wiped a tear from the corner of her eye. Inside, the TV blared an infomercial for cleaning products. She looked over her shoulder, as if the discount offers on grout cleaner and swivel-headed squeegees were too good to miss.

I didn't believe her and I had nothing to lose. 'Is she sick?' I said. 'Her phone's off.'

'She's not sick,' Mrs Nealon said firmly. 'She's fine. She – she's under a lot of pressure with the Leaving Cert. She needs a rest cure, that's all. I'm sorry, Ben, but now's really not the time.'

Reluctantly, I let it go. 'Tell her – tell her I said sorry.'

Mrs Nealon looked at me, a single tear trickling down her face inch by inch. Then she nodded, just once, pressed her tissue to her face and shut the door.

11

THE MEANING
OF FAMILY

I could've stayed at home every night and played video games by myself, but it just reminded me how much I missed Chelsea's company. I missed her stories about work, the way she gave out to me for always being on my phone, and the way she fell asleep with a cigarette in her hand, smoke dissolving into the air like the dreams behind her flickering eyelids. I couldn't tolerate cigarette smoke from anyone else, but it was part of the deal with Chelsea, so I didn't really mind.

When I got bored of flicking through my phone and chatting with Soda about how amazing Gary was, and had watched every Disney DVD at home at least twice, I found myself alone in PantiBar at 6 o'clock on a weekday, just to get out of the house. I'd never been to a gay bar on my own. It would've been terrifying if I'd never been there before, just sitting by myself trying not to catch the eye of some old man in case he thought I wanted company, but I knew PantiBar well enough for it to feel homely. I sipped a pint and surreptitiously checked out other guys while pretending to check my phone. I wasn't going to score anyone, but it was nice to look, and to remind myself that there were other men in the world besides nineteen-year-old closet cases with beefy biceps, dishevelled hair and the personality of a squashed tin can.

I made polite conversation with a drunk student who clumsily tried to chat me up, then mimed going for a smoke to get away from him, spending five minutes gulping fresh air outside while gangs of smokers waved their cigarettes around. An older guy jogged my elbow on the way back to the bar, and he looked as if he was going to talk to me, but I just smiled and nodded and walked on. Faced with the infinite variety of glittering drinks behind the mirrored bar, I stuck to beer, because it lasts longer, and I didn't want to go home just yet.

Panti herself was pulling pints for her customers, in a foot-high blonde wig, sparkly red dress and enough make-up to ruin your bedsheets forever.

She did a double-take as she served me my pint.

'There you go, chicken. Say, aren't you a friend of Miss Ugg

Lee? Where has that queen *been*? I haven't seen her skinny ass in *ages*.'

'She's hanging out with her new boyfriend. She met him here, actually, during her act. So, here I am ...'

'Don't tell me you're on your *own*?'

'Yeah.'

The music changed to a disco number. The lights spun around, gold and red, casting a glow across the grinning faces, the heaving bodies, the hands holding drinks above the crowd as the song kicked in and everyone rose up as one.

'Well, then, I have one piece of advice for you, kid,' Panti said, leaning down from on high like a minor goddess.

I held my breath. I could really use some good advice.

'Get out of my pub!' Panti said, in a theatrical accent straight out of *EastEnders*. 'Go find your friends, or a nice lad who isn't too drunk or already married, and stop moping around like a lost kitten. You're young, you're hot, you seem like a nice kid, and unlike *me*,' she added, pressing a finger to her red pout, 'you don't have the secret to eternal youth, glamour and fabulosity. So, use it while you can! Now, who was looking for a pint of vodka and Red Bull? Bruno's going to be busy with the mop later on, I can tell you ...'

I drank my pint and watched everyone else dirty dancing to disco tunes.

The drag act was Soda's ex-boyfriend Gavin – or, to give him his working title, Bet Down.

'Two drag queens in one relationship,' Soda had muttered one night after one too many white wine spritzers, clawing his face with fake nails. 'What was I thinking? Borrowing each other's wigs, tightening each other's corsets, tucking each other's –'

'Soda.'

'– but the *tantrums!* There I was, rising through the ranks, and of course Gavin got so bitterly jealous that he slashed my best frock backstage one night as I made my encore.'

'It was PantiBar's basement on a Tuesday night, Soda, not the Met Gala.'

'You sound just like him, darling. Bitter. Jealous. Envious of my success.'

'Wait, he slashed your best frock?'

'From shoulder to ankle.'

'Last time you told this story, you said he *took a slash* on your best frock.'

'Girl, why are we still talking about that loser? Let's forget it ever happened. He's a pizza delivery boy in the midlands now, who only comes up to Dublin on the quietest nights of the year. If you ever find yourself at one of his acts, make sure you boo him for me!'

Well, I clapped along with everyone else, but then I decided to go home. Panti was right. What I really needed was someone to talk to.

I kept my earphones in all the way home on the bus, nodding to the beat as the bus rattled around corners, wobbled on its wheels and threatened to fall apart at any second – but it didn't. Like most things in Dublin, the bus was on the verge of a nervous breakdown, but the collective will of the passengers held it together, barely. As we rounded the corner into our estate, I saw Aaron in his bedroom window, glaring at me over the 'Vote No!' poster he still had stuck up. For a moment he was frozen in time, framed there with the homophobic poster below his face, as he looked into my eyes, his mouth hanging open, as if he couldn't quite believe this was reality. Then the bus lurched around the corner, and he was gone.

At home, I found Mum on her favourite armchair, legs tucked underneath her, doing paperwork, as usual.

'Hey, Mum. Want a cup of tea?'

'Oh, go on,' she said, folding up the paperwork, taking off her reading glasses and rubbing her eyes. 'I've had enough to do for one day. We had to organise a counselling session for Noreen. The mum's boyfriend left her.'

I put the kettle on and dropped a couple of teabags into the pot. 'Poor Noreen. She'll get over it, though.'

'I worry about that child, but she's getting the best help we can give her. Sure, what can you do?'

I didn't know what to do about Noreen, but there was one problem I could tackle straight away. I'd been putting it off for too long. I made Mum's tea just the way she liked it, with half a sugar and just a drop of milk, and carried it over as she flicked on the TV. People in *Coronation Street* and *EastEnders* had embarrassing family problems all the time, so why should we be any different?

I took a deep breath and blurted everything out in one go.

'I'm worried about Aaron McAnally,' I said. 'He's the one who painted the graffiti on our wall. He's been acting weird at school too – he hasn't done anything, not really, but I think he might.'

Mum's eyes grew wide over the brim of her mug. 'What's he been doing?'

'He swung a baseball bat at me.'

'In the school grounds?'

'I was in the classroom. It was through the window.'

'So it wasn't actually in person?'

'Well, no.'

Mum put down her mug and took my hand. I only realised how upset I was when I felt my hand trembling under hers.

'Look,' she said. 'I know you had a hard time in school, but you can't let yourself feel like a victim. Aaron hasn't actually done anything, has he? I pulled strings to get you that job, so make the most of it. It'll help you later on, so stop imagining the worst that might happen and get on with it. It's not like when I was young. Things are so much better nowadays.'

I took my hand away.

'I know that,' I said. 'But sometimes it's hard to really feel it.'

'Don't be so dramatic,' Mum said. 'Go see what your sister's up to. She's up in her room, glued to her phone, as usual. Nathan will be home soon. Don't forget about dinner.'

'OK,' I said, even though I felt like Mum didn't really get it. This was why I needed Chelsea and Soda to talk to. So much for sharing my feelings.

I went up to Jamie's room and knocked on the door. She was sprawled on her bed, flicking through her phone.

'You look miserable,' she said. 'Did your boyfriend dump you?'

'He wasn't my boyfriend.'

'Poor Ben.'

'Never mind me,' I said, sitting down on the edge of the bed. 'What's up with you?'

'Nothing. I'm just looking at new trainers online. Do you think Dad would buy me another pair? These old things are knackered.'

'Of course he would. He dotes on you.'

'He dotes on you more,' Jamie said, as if it was a simple matter of fact. 'He's always asking you about your boyfriends and plans for college and stuff.'

'I don't have boyfriends! Anyway, that's not true. He's just trying to make it like there's no difference between us. You're his real kid, you know what I mean?'

'You're his real kid too, silly. Are these trainers cool?' Jamie held out her phone and showed me a pair of very sparkly shoes.

'I don't know. They're OK, I guess?'

'How come I get the only gay brother in the world who doesn't understand fashion?' Jamie said, shaking her head. 'Fail.'

I leaned back on one elbow. 'You've been acting all moody lately. What's up with you?'

Jamie put her phone down. I can't always read my baby sister's face. She's shy, she's private and she keeps things so bottled up inside that you're not always sure she's feeling any-thing – but the feelings come out eventually, like that time I found her crying on her own a week after her hamster died.

'Did Mum and Dad say something to you?'

'Nope.'

Jamie visibly relaxed, and I remembered how I'd felt when

I was Jamie's age, and had first started thinking about kissing boys, and being terrified that people could tell.

'How do you know if a boy likes you?' she said, twirling a strand of her hair and looking at the floor.

'Are we talking about a particular boy, or boys in general?'

'Um. Boys in general?'

'Sure, if you say so. Well, the important thing to remember is that boys are dumb, so if they like you, they usually try to get your attention by showing off.'

'Then he definitely likes me.'

'Smart guy.'

Jamie clambered over the bed and gave me a hug. 'Don't worry,' she said. 'Some other boy will like you again, even if you don't know anything about clothes.'

'Thanks,' I said, hugging her back. 'You really know how to cheer me up.'

We hung out in Jamie's bedroom until Mum called us downstairs.

Nathan was making his famous lemon sponge cake, the baking smells from the oven already filling the kitchen and living-room, which Mum had knocked into one big room when we first moved in. It's cosier that way, because Mum and Nathan are both good cooks. Even when he's just making pasta for dinner, like he was planning to now, it had to be something prepared from scratch, not out of a jar. Mum was watching one of her soaps, and Jamie bounced into the kitchen to help Nathan with the dinner, while I threw myself down on the sofa with a thumbs-up at Mum. She saw Jamie smiling and gave me the thumbs-up back.

'Can I make the syrup for the cake?' Jamie said.

'Sure. Just squeeze one and a half lemons, pour the juice into this saucepan, and stir in the icing sugar – I have the right amount ready on the counter.'

'What's for dinner?' she said, grabbing a lemon.

'Pasta with creamy mustard sauce and sausage. So, look, you skin the sausages, drop them in the pan with a little olive oil, and the meat starts to cook straight away.'

'It still looks pink.'

'Don't worry, it's cooking. So, I'll add a glass of white wine to the pan, then you'll take another glass to your mum, because she's had a hard day – haven't you, love?'

'Well, maybe just a little glass,' Mum said, and I took her tea mug from her good hand so Jamie could give her the glass of wine. She was comfortably curled up on the sofa with her work half-forgotten. On the telly, some greasy-looking man was yelling at some woman with a fake-fur jacket, because she thought she was too good for him now. 'She was always too good for you,' Mum said to the telly, sipping her wine.

Back in the kitchen, Nathan was teaching Jamie how to cook.

'See the way the wine is bubbling and some of the sausage is sticking to the pan? That's what you want. So, a pinch of chilli flakes and a handful of thyme, mix it in well. How's the syrup coming along?'

'All the sugar has melted. It smells amazing. Like sweets.'

'You can turn the heat off, and let it stand on one of the cool rings until the cake's out of the oven. Should be about ready.'

Nathan peered into the oven, one hand swathed in a giant oven-glove that made him look like a cartoon monster, and lifted out the cake. He has a special little cake tester with a pink plastic heart on top that Mum bought him, and he poked the cake with it, right down the middle, to see if it was baked all the way through.

'Perfect. We'll let it cool till after dinner. Now, how's the pasta looking?'

Jamie peeked under the lid of the bubbling pot, poking the pasta tubes with an experimental fork, then speared one and chewed it thoughtfully.

'Another minute or two. It's not past chewy yet.'

'OK, we'll try not to overcook it – you don't want limp pasta. So, back to the sauce. The thyme adds flavour, the mustard and chilli make it hot, the wine adds body and brings the flavours together with the meat, but it's the cream that binds everything together and makes it all work as a dish. So, we tip in the pot of cream, stir it all up, then you all sit down at the table, and I'll have it ready in two minutes flat.'

Nathan served dinner in the big orange bowls he likes best, with crusty bread and butter in a pile in the middle of the table. Before he tucked into his own dinner, he made holes in the lemon cake with the cake tester, then poured on the syrup, letting it sink in and drench the sponge, making it moist and sticky. The pasta was hot, a little bit spicy, but comforting too. Jamie wolfed down her food as if she hadn't a care in the world, and Mum beamed at me across the table when Jamie wasn't looking. The food started to soak up the beer I'd had in PantiBar, and I helped myself to more bread, because being sober now, when everyone was happy, was much better than feeling drunk and sorry for myself.

After dinner, Jamie curled up with Mum on the sofa, Mum's arm wrapped around her shoulder, because Jamie is still such a kid in lots of ways.

I gave Nathan a hand with the washing up.

'Hey, what's up with Chelsea lately?' he said. 'I haven't seen her around in ages. You guys didn't fall out, did you? I kind of miss the sound of her big, heavy boots stomping up and down the stairs, and the cigarette smoke your mum pretends she can't smell.'

'Hey, I don't smoke! That's Chelsea. I don't know. Mrs Nealon says she's taking a rest cure to get through her exams, whatever that means.'

I sneaked a look at Nathan's face, which had turned unusually serious as he rinsed Jamie's favourite glass under the tap.

'Is she depressed?'

'I – I don't know.'

Nathan shook his head sadly. 'It's a terrible thing,' he said, almost like he was talking to himself. 'Did she try to do something stupid? After a row you had, maybe?'

A sudden cold fear drenched me from top to toe, like when you hop in the shower before the water has warmed up. People always say 'do something stupid' when they really mean 'try to kill themselves', as if saying it more gently takes the blunt edge off an attempted suicide.

I shook my head and took Jamie's favourite glass from Nathan's hand. 'She wouldn't do that.'

Nathan was staring out the window, but not really looking at anything, as if he was lost in thought or remembering something.

'Nathan?'

'Sorry, Ben, I was miles away,' he said, picking up the next glass. 'Listen, I don't know, I'm only thinking out loud. She's doing her Leaving, isn't she? It's a stressful time. She'll be in touch when she wants to borrow some notes, don't worry.'

'She won't answer her phone and she's gone off Instagram.'

Nathan sighed. 'Well, you're her best friend. She'd tell you, wouldn't she, if anything was wrong?'

Soda's voice popped into my head, the words I'd been pretending I'd never heard. *Chelsea's in love with you. She's been in love with you, like, forever.*

Nathan passed me one of the heavy orange bowls and I began to rub it dry.

'She'd probably tell me, yeah. Unless … I don't know. It was something embarrassing. Or too personal.'

'Maybe she likes you in a way you don't like her back,' Nathan said lightly, or with an attempt at being light. He was very deliberately looking the other way.

'I don't know about that.'

'Well, it's not your fault, OK? Or hers either. We like who we like, and we hope they like us back, and the rest is luck.'

I concentrated very hard on drying the heavy orange bowl, because I knew Nathan was right.

Outside the kitchen window, right above the sink, the evening sky was turning pink, as our neighbours' washing flapped in the breeze.

'So,' Nathan said, 'how are things with the guy you've been dating, huh?'

I became convinced a stubborn piece of burned-in sausage meat just wouldn't shift.

'I had to break it off,' I said. 'It wasn't going to work out.'

'Aw, Ben,' Nathan said, putting down the fork he'd been scrubbing with a sponge that was on its last squeeze. 'I'm so sorry. I've been saying all the wrong things tonight.'

'Don't be silly,' I said. 'Dinner was awesome. You can't be good at everything.'

'Well, I'm glad you're wise enough to know when something's not going to work out. You'll find a guy who deserves you, don't worry. That's the smart son I raised,' Nathan said, running a hand over my stubbly head.

'Thanks, Dad,' I said, without even thinking about it. Nathan stopped rubbing my hair and just stared at me for what seemed like ten hours but was probably just two seconds. I could feel the sudden silence in the room, even as on the TV the woman in the fake-fur jacket was begging the greasy-looking man to give her one more chance. I just knew Mum and Jamie were staring at my back in shock. Then Nathan – nah, Dad – broke into a big wide grin that almost split his face in half, and gave me a hug.

'You'll be OK, kid,' he said. 'Plenty more sausage down the

butcher's, right?'

'*Nathan*,' Mum said in horror, covering one of Jamie's ears and pressing her head to her chest, 'not in front of Jamie!' But me and Dad just laughed, and finished doing the washing up as the sun set softly on the horizon.

12

THE COMPLAINT

My family is pretty boring, and that's OK. After dinner, we watched a bunch of people marching on TV, protesting against a tax on using water. Mum says it's because they don't want to pay for something that's always been free before. She's got strong opinions after a couple of glasses of wine.

'Our taxes pay for their dole money,' Mum said. 'But they think that's a right, too.'

'That's the price you pay for civilisation,' Dad said. 'Peaceful protest. Workers pay taxes. We all have a social safety net if you can't pay your own way.'

'I'm not talking about people who can't pay their own way. I'm talking about people who don't want to.'

'Right, right. But some people just find it hard to function in society, don't they? What are we meant to do? Let them die in the street?'

'No, but they can do something useful, instead of throwing rocks at cars and yapping because there's another bill to pay. We all have bills to pay. Some of us earn money to pay bills, and some of us, naming no names, expect it to be handed to us for free.'

'Why don't we just do away with money?' Jamie said. 'Just give everybody what they need?'

'Because there'd be freeloaders everywhere,' Mum said, 'getting away with doing nothing, while other people did all the hard work, keeping society ticking over. And mark my words, it would be the women doing all the work, while the men sat around drinking, and gambling, and talking about the meaning of life.'

'Hey, I made dinner!' Dad said.

'Yeah,' Mum said, 'but you're one in a million.'

Then Mum and Dad smooched on the sofa, while me and Jamie pretended to barf on the carpet.

Mum came up for air to drink more wine, and Dad lay back on the sofa, rubbing her feet. I turned off my phone, because I kept automatically checking to see if Chelsea had been in touch, but she hadn't, and it was getting depressing. Also, I didn't want to get any more messages from Thomas. I needed a break from dating and drama.

'See,' Dad said, 'I don't mind seeing protestors out protesting. It means society is working, on some level. There might be problems, but at least you can do something about it. You never know. The government might even listen.'

'Like with the gay marriage referendum,' I said. It was only the first of July, but already it felt like the marriage referendum back in May had made history.

'Like the whole gay rights movement,' Dad said. 'You know, that all started with a black trans woman hitting a policeman with her high heel because he was trying to shut down a gay bar. And he was only doing his job, because that was the law.'

'What's a trans woman?' Jamie said.

'A girl who grew up in a boy's body, but it always felt wrong – sometimes, trans people have an operation to change. But anyway, people decided the law around gay people had to be changed, and that's how the world gets more fair and tolerant.'

'By hitting a policeman with a shoe?' I said.

'Well, that's one way to do it,' Dad said.

'We do *not* hit policemen with shoes,' Mum said, hitting Dad with her shoe.

'Ouch! Well, maybe sometimes we ought to. That's all I'm saying. I wish more people would hit policemen with shoes back home in Jamaica. It might knock some sense into them.'

'What's so bad about Jamaica?' Jamie said.

'Nothing,' Dad said, 'unless, say, you happen to be gay. Oh, boy. That's not cool. You know, I don't think I ever told you about my cousin Cedric, did I? Well, he grew up back home in the same town that I did. Our mums were sisters, and we were raised all right, but Cedric never was like the other boys, you know? His dad called him a sissy, and he tried to knock it out of him, and not with a shoe. With his fists. With a belt. *It's for his own good*, he'd say. *How's he going to grow up into a fine young man and give me grandchildren if he wants to dress like a woman and talk like a woman and act like a woman in bed?*'

'*Nathan!*' Mum said, like she always does when he even remotely refers to anything to do with sex in front of Jamie, as if she doesn't know how she got here.

'I'm only saying what he said. Come on, they're old enough. The thing was, what did any amount of battering do except make Cedric ashamed of himself, and hurt his mother too?'

'Why?' Jamie said, but I could guess why. I knew how Mum had always looked out for me, worried that I was being bullied because I was different.

'Because she couldn't protect him,' Dad said. 'It's people like my uncle who make things bad for kids like Cedric, but they dress it up as love and concern.'

'What happened to Cedric?' Jamie said.

'Oh,' Nathan said, getting up off the sofa, so we couldn't see his face. He pretended to tidy up things on the coffee table that didn't need to be tidied. 'He died … But that was a long time ago. Hey, who's ready for lemon syrup cake?'

But the lemon syrup cake tasted a bit sad once I'd heard about Cedric. We watched a dumb film on Netflix, and Jamie fell asleep on Mum's lap. The film was a romantic comedy, where the guy and the girl end up together, even though they hate each other to begin with. I wondered if that ever happened in real life, but I didn't think so. If you liked someone, you'd probably know it from the start. Later, as Mum screwed the top back on whatever was left of the wine and made mugs of cocoa for me and her and Dad, I helped carry Jamie upstairs to bed.

'How did Cedric die?' I whispered, as Dad tucked Jamie in, switching on the pink bedside lamp she still liked to have on in case she woke up in the middle of the night.

Dad sighed. 'Well,' he said. 'You're old enough to know, so I might as well tell you. He took his own life. That was before I ever came to Ireland. Europe isn't paradise – and definitely not if you're black – but you can make a happy life for yourself if you're lucky.'

'Poor Cedric,' I said.

I wondered what things would've been like for me if I'd been born a hundred years ago, or somewhere where they killed you for loving the wrong person. Jamie's bedside lamp cast a glow on her face, pink light pooling over her brown skin, gilding her eyelashes and the curls of her hair like sparkling stars.

Dad put his arm around me as we looked down at Jamie's sleepy face.

'I've been lucky,' he said, 'and all I want for my kids is that they know they're loved, and they can love whoever they like. OK?'

'I'm giving up on love,' I said. 'But thanks anyway.'

'It'll happen,' Dad said, and I wanted to believe him.

'Cocoa's ready!' Mum yelled, and we went downstairs, and made fun of Mum for being tipsy, and watched a documentary about long-distance dating while we drank our cocoa. It reminded me of one of Soda's stories.

Soda had once been in a long-distance relationship with Dave, a bisexual Londoner he'd struck up a friendship with on Fitlads.

'Mixed race,' Soda had explained. 'White English mother, Nigerian father. He was a lovely guy and he'd just broken up with his long-term girlfriend. I think he needed someone to talk to more than a boyfriend. Girl, he had so much *baggage*. It was only when he came to Dublin for the first time that he told me he had a seven-year-old daughter.'

They'd travelled back and forth between Dublin and London

on and off for a year, but Dave had made the mistake of saying *I love you* by text. Soda had told him not to be silly, they barely knew each other, though in the future, who knew what would happen? After that, Dave had cut off all communication and they'd never seen each other again.

'He was so good looking,' Soda had sighed, 'and a real gentleman. Maybe I should've said *I love you* and moved to London.'

'But you weren't in love with him.'

'I would've fallen in love with him,' Soda had insisted, 'gradually. His baby-mama might've died in a freak accident, and we could've adopted the seven-year-old daughter, living in perfect harmony. Post-racial. Post-sexual identity. Postcode W1.'

'Not so perfect for the mother of his child,' I'd said, making a mental note never to get embroiled in a long-distance relationship. As usual, I'd learned more from one of Soda's stories than I did from watching any amount of straight relationship advice on TV.

But then, some people – people like Cedric – didn't get the chance to make funny stories out of their romantic mistakes. We had to remember them and keep their stories alive.

Mum and Dad must've carried me up to bed too because I don't remember falling asleep. I remember Homework Club the next day, though, because it really did turn into the worst day ever. It started off OK. I had a meeting scheduled with Miss Murgatroyd because she wanted me to stay on for a month to help with administrative chores once the school year was over, so I made a special effort to arrive early and look smart. We sat in the canteen with fancy biscuits and cups of tea. Miss Murgatroyd's hand hovered over each of the biscuits in turn as we discussed the girls' progress.

'At the beginning of the year,' I said, 'Anna could barely read by herself. She had to sound out every letter and try to put them together in her head. But she was really determined to do her best, and it showed. She's not even afraid of doing sums any more. Back in October, she refused to look at a maths book, and now she's the first to get started every day.'

'That's because she wants to finish first and play with the toy farm set,' Miss Murgatroyd said, wiggling her fingers above a round biscuit in a gold foil wrapper. 'She's become obsessed with animals since we did that little trip to the farm and she asked lots of awkward questions about where milk came from. But her test results are very encouraging.'

'Noreen is way ahead of the other girls, but she was really teary one day last week. She wouldn't play with the other girls when she finished her homework – she just sat in the corner by herself, being sad. I didn't know what to do about it.'

'Don't worry about it,' said Miss Murgatroyd. 'I've never

really liked marzipan. Maybe a Garibaldi? Her counsellor says she's making progress. She just needs to get used to her new situation at home, and it helps that she has two older sisters. She'll come around. She's even becoming good friends with Anna, since they discovered a mutual interest in dance. It's helped her enormously.'

'They keep having competitions to see who can do the splits. Yesterday, Noreen asked me why boys don't like doing the splits, and Roxie whispered something in her ear. I didn't know where to look.'

'All a natural curiosity about growing up,' Miss Murgatroyd said. 'Ooh, I know! One of these triple-chocolate fudge cookies. Now, Jessica ...'

'Jessica is still the slowest, but she's made some progress. She just needs more attention than the others. But she still makes excuses to come up and do her homework at the desk beside me.'

'Yes,' Miss Murgatroyd said through a mouthful of crumbs. 'She definitely needs more attention. But remember, it can't be at the expense of the other girls. Ah! Got it.'

She beamed as she plucked a stray piece of fudge from her teeth, then stuck it back in her mouth and swallowed it. Mission accomplished, she looked at me and folded her hands on the table. 'As you know, I had to talk to Roxie's mother about her language in class the other day. I'm afraid something else has happened since then. She had a fight with another girl in class this morning. To make matters worse, it was Noreen.'

'Oh,' I said.

This was serious.

'I had to phone her mother at once, of course. Roxie claims that Noreen tried to touch her and she didn't like it, but really, Noreen was just trying to help her with her schoolbag, like they all do, every day.' Miss Murgatroyd paused to clear her throat. 'Then Roxie called her – there's no nice way to put this – a dyke, and slapped her in the face.'

I stared at Miss Murgatroyd in disbelief. 'That's horrible,' I said. 'Especially because Roxie's so bright. I mean, she's doing so well in class. When she reads, she's not just mouthing the words. She actually acts out the story ...' I trailed off, because that wasn't the point.

'This is her second school, Ben,' Miss Murgatroyd said gently. 'She was expelled for physical violence from the last one. We have to make it clear that her behaviour is unaccept-able, no matter how bright she is. Luckily, Noreen seems fine, but as she's been in counselling lately, we have to do everything to put her needs first.'

'Roxie must be picking up language like that at home,' I said. 'I'll try to give them all extra attention, to make it fair.'

Even as the words came out of my mouth, I couldn't help thinking about Aaron's head-to-head with Roxie's mum that day. I felt uneasy. Miss Murgatroyd just smiled and put a hand on my arm, as if I'd said something sad but didn't know it. When she turned away, I wiped the crumbs from her hand off my sleeve and helped myself to another biscuit before the day's work began. If it was going to be one of those days, I'd need more of Granny's cure-all to get through it.

After the meeting, Miss Murgatroyd had paperwork to do, as it was coming up to the end of the school year. I began to set up the classroom with enough number cubes, pencils and lunches for that day's Homework Club – or at least, that was the plan. The summer holidays were looming, and the girls weren't really in a homework sort of mood. Anna danced and Noreen tried to lift her up, then Roxie pointed to Noreen and mouthed 'Gay!' Then Roxie sneaked Jessica's favourite rubber up her sleeve and pretended she couldn't find it, even when Jessica started crawling around on her tummy under the table.

'Noreen, put Anna down. Sit on your chairs, please, girls. Roxie, I know you have Jessica's rubber up your sleeve. Jessica, stop crawling around like a hamster and sit on your chair properly. Anna, no sulking, thank you. Heads up. We have to start our homework.'

'Ben, I had a pet hamster, so I did,' said Noreen. 'But it didn't crawl around on its belly, so it didn't. It lay on its back with its four paws up in the air. It was dead!'

Anna threw herself on the floor with her four paws up in the air, mimicking the death of a hamster. Jessica laughed and forgot she was underneath a table and bumped her head trying to stand up. Roxie sneaked the rubber out of her sleeve when she thought I wasn't looking and put it underneath Noreen's pencil case.

'I think *Noreen* has Jessica's rubber,' she said.

'I don't have her rubber,' Noreen said hotly. 'Look!' She lifted her pencil case and the rubber was there, pink and half used, like chewed bubblegum. 'I never took it!' Noreen wailed, and Roxie allowed herself a smug smile before turning innocent eyes to mine.

'She *did* have it,' Roxie said.

'I didn't,' said Noreen.

'What noise does a dead hamster make?' said Anna.

'Wait,' said Jessica, plonking herself on her chair and rubbing her head. 'Where's my rubber?'

'Anna, chair. Noreen, I know you didn't take the rubber. Roxie, it doesn't matter where the rubber was, because it's back now. Jessica, there's your rubber. OK? Let's start.'

'Ben, Ben,' Roxie said. 'We were all in dance class this week, and Anna learned how to twirl on her toes, and Noreen learned hip-hop dancing, and Jessica doesn't know how to dance, do you, Jessica?'

'What?' said Jessica.

Miss Murgatroyd shot me a sympathetic smile from her desk in the corner.

'You'd like dance class, Ben,' Roxie said. 'All the dance teachers are boys and they're all gay, so they are. Ben should marry one of the dance teachers!'

'I don't want to marry anyone,' I said. 'There's only one thing I'm married to, and that's homework.'

Secretly, I was unnerved that seven-year-olds were plotting to manage my love life.

'Look, Ben, look!' Roxie said, leaping out of her chair and tumbling across the floor. 'I learned how to stand on my hands!'

Roxie did a handstand at the exact same moment her mother flung open the door. She stood in the doorway with wild eyes and her hair flung back, skinny legs encased in tight black leggings, a pink jumper falling off one shoulder. Her eyes were bright and angry as they flashed around the room. She barely looked at me. The hand clutching the doorknob was white around the knuckles.

'Roxie! Stop showing everyone your knickers! Miss Murgatroyd, come here, you. I have something to say to you, so I do, and I don't care who hears it.'

'Miss Beaumont,' said Miss Murgatroyd, sweeping up her skirt and gliding across the floor with more grace than I'd ever be able to muster, no matter how many dance instructors I married, 'I can't speak to you here, I'm afraid. Come into my office if you'd like to chat.'

'I don't want to chat, I want your head on a plate! Roxie. Come here. We're leaving. See her?' she said, pointing an accusatory finger at Miss Murgatroyd. 'Don't you listen to a word she says. In our house, if someone touches us, we hit them back. You hear me?'

'Yes, Mum,' Roxie said, clutching her schoolbag to her chest.

'Miss Beaumont, this is very irregular,' Miss Murgatroyd said. 'You can't just walk in here and –'

'Yes, I can,' said Roxie's mum triumphantly. 'I just did, didn't I? This school is a disgrace. No wonder my child is picking up bad habits. Well, not any more. I'm pregnant again, I don't need this stress, and I'm taking my daughter out of Homework Club!'

Roxie's mum trembled in the doorway like an indignant flamingo.

Roxie pulled the sleeves of her coat over her arms.

Miss Murgatroyd drew herself up to her full height. 'Noreen did *not* touch Roxie,' she said. 'And even if she had –'

'If my daughter says she did, then she did. Tell us all what happened, Roxie?'

Roxie raised her face from the floor and whispered, 'Noreen touched me.'

'See? That's what happened. I don't teach my daughter to lie, but I do teach her to defend herself. Now get your bloody coat on, Roxie, I can't stand here all day!'

Miss Murgatroyd took a deep breath. 'As I explained to you on the phone,' she said, 'that's *not* what happened.'

'I'm making a complaint to the board of management,' Roxie's mum said, looking everywhere except at me. 'You can say what you like, but having a *gay* in the classroom goes against the Catholic ethos of this school, and it's having a negative effect on the well-being of my child.'

And with that, she flounced out, Roxie trailing behind her, red in the face.

There was a horrible silence.

I couldn't help being impressed with Roxie's mum's sense of the dramatic. She knew how to make an exit. She was a loss to Mum's favourite soaps. At the same time, her words had sounded rehearsed, and that was bad.

She really was going to lodge a complaint. Somehow, I felt weirdly calm.

Her head-to-head with Aaron finally made sense.

'Well,' Miss Murgatroyd said, breaking the silence, 'that

wasn't very nice.' She found her chair and sat down.

'Are you OK?' I said. 'I'll make you a cup of tea, two sugars. And I'll get you another biscuit. My granny always says it's good for shock.'

'Yes, I think that would be ... Yes ... Thank you, Ben.' Miss Murgatroyd sat up straight in her chair. For the first time, I saw her as a steely-eyed principal. 'I must call the board of management. I'm afraid this could be quite serious.' I almost expected her to slam a fist on the desk, like a general declaring war.

'Tea first,' I said, as the kids all looked at each other, wide eyed and silent.

Even they knew something adult and dangerous was going on.

'OK, girls,' I said. I felt shaken, but I didn't want to show it, so it was better to keep busy and focus on the job. 'Sorry about the shouting. I think Roxie's mum is just a bit upset.'

'I don't think Roxie's very happy,' Jessica said.

'Shush,' said Noreen, 'we're not allowed to talk about it.'

'My mum gives me hugs,' said Anna. 'Every night.'

'I bet Roxie's mum doesn't give her hugs,' Jessica said.

Noreen put her hands over her ears, and Anna put her hands over Jessica's mouth.

'Well,' I said, 'that's between Roxie and her mum, isn't it? Now, who wants cheese and crackers?'

Everyone's hands flew in the air, because no matter how bad things get, there's always lunch.

Miss Murgatroyd took me aside as the kids tucked in. 'This is awkward, Ben,' she said. 'But I have to let you know that having someone of your sexuality in a position of authority at a Catholic school is something of a grey area, legally speaking, in Ireland. If Miss Beaumont makes a complaint and it's upheld, well …'

Time slowed down as Miss Murgatroyd's words dangled in the air.

'You mean, I could lose my job?' I hoped my voice wouldn't crack. It already sounded weird in my own ears.

'I hope not,' Miss Murgatroyd said, laying a hand gently on my arm.

'But what about college?' I said. 'I'm supposed to be starting teacher training in September.'

'Let's see what happens,' Miss Murgatroyd said, and I felt the future that had seemed so certain melt away in front of me. 'And I want you to know, I'll do everything I can.'

Numb, but needing something to do, I left the classroom to make tea.

It was so unfair! And to make it worse, Roxie had always secretly been my favourite. Yes, she was the naughtiest girl in Homework Club, but she was also the brightest. On the days when she wasn't showing off, she was actually learning, and you could see her making progress – the satisfaction of learning new words, the sudden joy when a maths problem made sense – week after week. I stood outside the kitchen, looking at the kids' paintings on the wall. One was by Roxie, a colourful daub that captured the Homework Club family – her, Noreen, Jessica and Anna standing in a circle around me, Ben, with a bigger smile than anyone could have in real life, holding a book, with stickers of hearts and butterflies all around us. One thing I hadn't told Miss Murgatroyd was that one day, when Miss Murgatroyd had been out with toothache after one stray chickpea too many, I'd explained that their teacher was visiting her dentist.

'I don't like visiting the dentist,' Roxie had said. 'He's always telling you not to eat sweets.'

'Well, maybe he's right,' I'd said. 'But Miss Murgatroyd's dentist is a woman.'

Roxie's eyes had grown wide. 'I didn't know a girl could be a dentist!'

'A girl can be anything she wants to be,' I'd said.

'Wow,' Roxie said. 'That's amazing. I want to be a frog!'

OK, so she'd spent the rest of the day hopping around, ribbiting and pretending to catch flies, but it was still a good memory.

And now, after a whole school year of Homework Club, I

might not get to be a teacher after all – because some folks still didn't think gay people should be allowed to be whatever they wanted to be.

That was when Roxie came racing back down the corridor as her mum yelled her name.

'Roxie! Come back here, you!'

Roxie threw herself around my legs.

There were tears in her eyes.

'Goodbye, Ben,' she said, giving me a big hug. 'I don't care who you marry, OK?'

And then she was gone.

13

TECHNOLOGY CAN MAKE YOU FEEL SO ALONE

For the next two weeks, it seemed like everyone was in love except me, and I knew it because they kept telling me on social media. Couples posted selfies in the park, lying on the grass with the guts of a picnic between them, smiling at each other's faces while one of them raised an arm and captured the spontaneous moment of joy, before putting the image through a hazy sunset filter to make the Irish weather look better than it really was, hashtag couple, hashtag happy, hashtag love. Every couple who'd been together for more than five minutes kept reminding me of their anniversaries, with captions like 'This guy!' and the heart-eyed emoji, with photos and check-ins from every date they'd ever had. Even Twitter was full of friends-of-friends flirting with each other, before sliding into each other's DMs, away from my jealous gaze. They would reappear a week or so later, together in real life this time, with a photograph of them both laughing over the misspelt name on their takeaway Starbucks Grande Caramel Macchiatos.

I spent more time than was healthy checking other people's relationship statuses online. If you've ever been the singleton in your friendship group, you know how it is. One night you're mouthing all the words as your drag queen friend lip-syncs onstage, then fast-forward a few weeks, and you're standing on your own at the side of the dance floor, watching everybody pair off, wishing you had a strong enough Wi-Fi signal to order pizza for one and a taxi home. My dream guy had been living a lie, my best friend had gone AWOL, I was about to lose my job, and I couldn't even get a date. What's the point of having marriage equality if no one wants to take you out for a pint in PantiBar, and maybe a snog in Burger King afterwards?

My life was turning into that part of the film where the hero walks through a montage, passing a happy couple in the park, nuking a microwave meal for one, opening a beer in his empty apartment, kneeling by the toilet bowl surrounded by empty bottles and, finally, waking up on the sofa, clutching the cherished memento of his last relationship, pondering the meaning of life. His phone shows zero messages. He sinks back on the sofa. He's been defeated by life itself.

It's not that I wasn't happy for Soda and Gary. Of course I was. They'd beaten the odds. Soda was a drag queen who'd found a man comfortable enough in his own skin to take on Soda's inner diva for who she was, and I wished them all the luck in the world. It was just that I hadn't seen that much of Soda for the last month, not since he'd started staying over in Gary's place every other night, and I missed the way we used to talk about all the awful dates he used to have, and all the potential dates I might go on.

'Don't worry, Ben,' Soda said one rare evening when we got to grab a coffee and catch up. 'You're young. You'll find the right guy, eventually.'

'Even if I have to wait till I'm twenty-five?'

'I'm not twenty-five yet! Good God, girl. Being single is turning you mean.'

'Life's not all about getting a boyfriend.'

'Said the spinster in the corner.'

'Shut up, Soda. Don't be that friend. Don't be that friend who, as soon as he gets a boyfriend, starts to pity all the single pals he never sees any more. I suppose you're too busy giving him sloppy lovebites after dinner to think about lads online any more, never mind me.'

Soda put down his cappuccino, sank back in his squashy armchair, and peered at me over the rim of his coffee cup. He folded his arms and put his head to one side, examining me like an exhibit in the zoo.

'You. Are. Jealous,' he said.

I sipped my herbal tea.

Herbal tea always smells better than it tastes. It was red, it smelled like berries and forests and, when you swirled it in your cup, it looked as deep as the hope that welled up in your heart when your online crush approached you in a bar and said 'Hi!' But then you tasted it, and it was thin and bitter and not very nice, just like your online crush when you finally had a conversation.

'No, I'm not,' I said. 'I'm happy for you. But what about me?'

'You're totally jealous. I can see it in your big, blue Western eyes. Don't lie to me, girl. They're over-spilling with emotion. It's the weakness of the white race. You just don't have my Oriental inscrutability. What am I thinking right now?'

I gazed into Soda's face. 'You're thinking about how much you want to buy me a beer,' I said. 'You're thinking, poor Ben, he looks like he could really use some alcohol. Let's find a bar and judge some lads over three pints of whatever's cheapest.'

'Wrong,' said Soda. 'First of all, I'm thinking you're a massive racist for not contradicting all that Oriental inscrutability crap. Secondly, I'm thinking how you're suddenly all me, me, me. Snap out of it! There's only room for one diva in this friendship, and that's *me*. You should be asking yourself, what's best for Soda? And right now, what's best for Soda is having an awesome boyfriend who actually likes me. It's so weird. You know what I'm really thinking? I'm really thinking how nice it is to be the person someone else is jealous of for a change. Oh, come on. Cheer up. Be happy for me!'

'I am,' I said, putting down my tea, but not quite ready to admit to myself that it was actually horrible. 'I just miss hanging out with you. My life sucks right now. I can't get a date, there's been a complaint about me at work and, worst of all, Chelsea's disappeared. I don't know what's going on with her. My folks think she tried to kill herself, and now she's in the loony bin or something.'

'Well, why don't they do something about it?'

'Like what? They tried going next door with a bottle of wine for a chat, but Chelsea's parents clammed up and wouldn't talk about it.'

'No one is less likely to end up in the loony bin than Chelsea. If Gary ever throws me over for some queen with a twenty-eight-inch waist and bigger hair, I'll probably go completely insane. I won't be responsible for my actions. I'll murder them both with a stiletto.'

'Yeah, but at least you can channel all the emotional pain into an epic lip-sync. Some of us have to drown our sorrows with cheesy romantic comedies on Netflix. Last night I shared a bottle of rosé with my mum.'

'That's what I like about you, Ben. Your tragicomic attempts at dating make me feel so much better about myself. At least I had a boyfriend at your age.'

'But that was so long ago. Times have changed. We have technology now, like mobile phones, and the internet, and the endless possibilities of discovering new romantic partners all around the globe. Remember?'

'Yeah,' Soda said, picking up his cappuccino and sipping off the foam. 'How's that working out for you?'

'Pretty terrible.'

'Might be time to take a break from all that,' Soda said.

'Yeah,' I said. 'Oh, I have one piece of good news. Aaron finally took the "Vote No!" poster out of his bedroom window. I noticed from the bus stop yesterday.'

'Girl,' Soda said, 'you should not be staring in his bedroom window. I'm glad he's moving with the times, but the last thing you need is a restraining order. Hey, I know what'll cheer you up. A juicy piece of gossip about one of my exes. Remember Kyle?'

'Unemployed stoner? Dreamy eyes? Sculpted abs?'

'And the package of an underwear model after he's stuffed an extra pair of socks down the front. Well, he's still working on his abs,' Soda said, 'except in prison. He got busted for drug dealing. I cut all contact. Is that bad?'

'Of course not. You have to protect yourself.'

'I had terrible taste in men before Gary. Oh, here he is now.'

'Hi, Ben,' said Gary, stumbling through the door of the coffee shop, looking ruggedly handsome and impossibly manly, maybe because he wasn't half a stone underweight and overly worried about his hair. He stooped down to kiss Soda on the cheek, then hunkered down beside him, with an arm draped casually around his boyfriend's shoulder. 'Seeing anyone these days?'

'I'm getting a coffee,' I said. 'This tea is horrible.'

'Look,' Soda said, 'you have to admit when something isn't working, and be ready to move on to the next option. It's just a shame dating isn't as easy as ordering a different coffee.'

'No word from that Peter guy?' Gary said, trying to be kind.

'He's being a nuisance,' I said. 'Don't ask. I'm trying to avoid him.'

I got myself a coffee, and Gary tactfully changed the subject.

Thomas was still pestering me. I was getting stupid texts from him every other day, saying things like 'Wow, just had a great coffee!' or 'Time for work, the struggle is real!' He even sent me a dick pic on Snapchat that I could've lived without. It was too much, so I didn't respond.

That's what made it extra awkward when I ran into him on the way back from coffee with Soda and Gary. Naturally, it was right across the road from the pub where we'd had our first date. Maybe the universe has a sense of humour, or maybe it just doesn't care about gay lads getting over their first broken heart.

'Hey, Ben,' Thomas said, right up in my face. 'Long time no see! You've gone quiet! Did you get my texts? What's up?'

He stood there, being all tall and attractive and annoying. He was wearing stubble like it was a fashion accessory, rather than something that just grew out of his face. He was grinning at me as if nothing had happened.

'Hey, Peter. Thomas. I meant Thomas.'

'Ah, come on, don't be like that,' he said, putting a hand on my shoulder.

I squirmed, but he just held it there. His eyes shone under thick black eyebrows that made him look like a wolf trying to decide what to have for dinner. He leaned in close and lowered his voice. 'Admit it. There's something a little bit exciting about me not being out, isn't there? You're cute, you know. Why else would I still be bothering when you're playing so hard to get?

There's no need to be so uptight. We could have a lot of fun, as long as it's in secret.'

'I'm not playing hard to get,' I said, shrugging his hand off my shoulder. 'I am hard to get. And when I decide who I want to be with, it won't be someone who wants us to be a secret.'

I left him standing there, looking puzzled and angry, stuck my earphones in, and forgot about Peter, or Thomas, or whatever his name was.

Taxis, prams, discount offers on six-packs of beer, beggars, junkies, kids walking home after school, an old man rolling a cigarette outside a supermarket, a woman getting highlights pasted on in a hairdresser's, dogs sniffing each other in the street, an ugly daub of graffiti that said 'Refugees Go Home', flags fluttering for football matches down the pub, flowers coming into bloom in window boxes high above the city, bodies pumping on treadmills behind the glass walls of a gym, a crusty-haired hippie handing out fliers for half-price cocktails, pizza sold in slices sweating slightly on rotating Perspex shelves, empty buildings staring blank-eyed at people walking by, posters, billboards, plants thrusting through the painted iron railings of vacant lots that were due to be developed into apartment blocks, and the weight of my phone in my pocket as music bleated through earphones and into my brain, telling me that life went on, both inside my head and outside in the real world, where everybody else was dealing with the business of being alive, too.

I was glad to get back to my estate, with its familiar front doors and normal stuff happening everywhere – piles of tools and bricks from the odd jobs dads hadn't finished yet, mums washing windows while the weather was good, a ginger tom-cat on the prowl, huge TV screens glowing on living-room walls, and the woman a few doors down sitting out in her wheelchair, watching the first butterfly of the season drunk-enly swim across her garden. All good, except the last person I wanted to see was sitting at the bus stop. He hopped out of the plastic seat to come running my way as I crossed the estate.

I felt my fists clench as Aaron McAnally came bounding over.

He mouthed something I couldn't hear, so I plucked my earphones out and stood still, watching him approach, my muscles tense and my heart rate jumping. I didn't want another fight. I tried not to look scared, but he didn't look angry or upset. His face went red as he stood in front of me, but he kept looking down at the ground, shuffling in his trainers. Then he stuck out a big paw.

'Um,' he said. 'I've been trying to get you at the school, but it's like you're avoiding me.'

He looked so pathetic, I almost laughed. 'Yeah,' I said. 'I wonder why?'

'Look,' he said, 'I'm sorry.'

'Sorry for what?' I said, relaxing a little and letting my guard down – but not too much.

'You know,' he said, his paw still stuck out for me to shake. 'All that stuff I said. And did.'

'What brought this on?'

'Don't leave me hanging here, man,' he said, looking up and waggling his hand about. 'I'm serious. I'm sorry. I was a dick-head, it wasn't cool, I won't do it again.'

I looked him up and down, trying to work out if it was some sort of trick. Truth was, he looked harmless, and embarrassed, his face twisted into a sorry expression, the red patches on his face matching the clammy hand he was holding out to me. Slowly, I took his hand, and we shook. I was half expecting him to make some stupid joke about AIDS and pull his hand away, but he didn't. He just breathed a big sigh of relief and sat down on the nearest neighbour's wall.

'I had a big row with Roxie's mum,' he said, 'after, you know, she made that complaint about you and everything. I didn't mean for it to go so far. I had no idea you could, like, actually lose your job. I feel bad.'

'Good,' I said.

'I mean, what's the big deal? I was always kind of like, ugh, gay boys, yuck, but then I thought about it, and I was like, well, hang on. It's not really any of my business, is it?'

'Fair point,' I said. 'But tell me, what *did* you think was going to happen?'

'Well,' Aaron said, running a hand over his head. 'I knew Roxie's mum was against the whole gay marriage thing. She used to talk to my parents about it. So I figured she'd make a complaint about you, like, being gay but working in a Catholic school and all.'

'Wow,' I said. 'Nice.'

'I know, I know,' Aaron said. 'Just listen. I know it was bad, but I never thought the school would *do* anything. I thought it would just make things awkward for you for, like, a day or two, and then go away.'

'Guess you were wrong,' I said.

'Yeah. Well. I was so pissed off about Killer and you punching me and everything. I wasn't thinking straight. I mean – I am straight – that's not what I meant!'

Aaron looked so panicked that I might've thought he was gay, it was actually funny.

'You idiot,' I said. 'I know you're straight, trust me. You're the straightest person in the world.'

'Right, yeah. Ha. Anyway. So I just thought, well, what's the harm in you teaching kids, anyway? That's a mad rule even for a Catholic school, when you think about it. Everyone needs a job. I don't have to like kissing fellas, and you don't have to like, I don't know, cheese and onion crisps or karate. I mean, we can both like different things, yeah? But it's kind of stupid to punch each other in the face about it.'

'OK.'

'Anyway,' Aaron said, standing up and scratching the back of his neck and looking me straight in the face without sneering, which was a first, 'that's what I think. So, you know … good luck and everything. I hope you find a nice boyfriend and stuff.'

'You're so weird.'

'I know. Don't tell anybody. They'll probably think I'm gay. Not that there's anything wrong with that,' he added quickly, 'but I'm not. Honest.'

'I believe you,' I said. 'Take it easy.'

And then Aaron nodded and walked off, looking happier and more confident than he had in a long time. It must feel good to learn how to think for yourself, at last.

I went home. It felt like Aaron was finally growing up, and that had to be a good thing. But it also felt like giving prejudiced people the power to take your job away was the real problem. And that was a problem that was bigger than me. I had to focus on the stuff I could change.

I could've signed up to all the dating apps that Soda used to like so much. I could've flirted my way around the globe, sending cute pics to people I'd never meet, or striking up remote friendships with guys who'd like my pictures back, but who'd never bring me breakfast in bed on a random Saturday morning. I could've gone on a date with one of the guys who were nice to me on Grindr, even if I wasn't interested, just for an ego boost, or a free pint, or something to do on a wet Wednesday. I could've flirted back with the guy I'd been to school with who had a girlfriend but kept sending me gym selfies, which I laughed off as banter, though I was pretty sure he wouldn't say no to a sneaky snog in the showers.

I wasn't feeling it, though.

I was pretty content with trying to teach kids maths, promising myself I'd study hard in college, watching loads of TV and, reluctantly, deleting Thomas's pics off my phone. That was the hardest part. It was as if Peter had existed in a film I'd seen once, and Thomas was just some annoying person I'd spend the rest of my life avoiding if I saw him in a bar. As far as I could see, the only upside to having dated a closet case was you weren't likely to run into him in PantiBar the next time you screwed up the courage to meet someone for a pint. Then again, maybe he just had his own growing up to do.

It was almost the summer holidays. Soon, my work experience would wind up, bar some paperwork for Miss Murgatroyd, if the board of management didn't fire me first, and there'd be eight glorious weeks of sunshine and cider to look forward to – and after that, I'd turn eighteen and start college. It seemed unreal that in one year's time, I'd be fretting over whether I'd revised enough, whether my grades were as good as they should be, and whether I'd had enough experience to know if teaching was still what I wanted to do. But I reckoned that if Roxie's mum's meltdown hadn't put me off teaching, nothing would. Hopefully the law would change soon, meaning schools wouldn't be able to fire gay teachers, and I could have the career I wanted without being afraid of losing my job or living in the closet, squashed in between Thomas and my banished pink polo shirt.

Mum had been great.

'We'll fight them all the way on this,' she said. 'And if they try to fire you, we'll sue.'

Maybe she didn't always get it, but it was good to know she was on my side.

Miss Murgatroyd told me to be patient, that school procedures took a long time because of all the paperwork, so I carried on teaching Noreen, Anna and Jessica, for now.

Maybe I wasn't ready to date anyone yet, but I felt like I'd grown up a lot since I'd finished school. I had grant application forms to fill in, and I was saving for a new laptop because I'd need it for college. I told myself I didn't have time for a boyfriend anyway, and put all my energy into working hard for the year ahead. When I was finished at Homework Club, when I was done with the extra admin duties, and when I'd submitted my forms, I'd allow myself to kick back and hang out more with Soda and Gary. I might even kiss a few guys, if they asked me nicely.

But there was one thing I still had to do before summer seduced me with meaningless pop songs, sunburned shoulders and stolen kisses in terrible nightclubs.

I checked Instagram, but she was still missing from it.

I rang the bookshop, but they told me she was on an extended leave of absence.

I knocked in next door, but her mum was weary, and her dad was angry, and I couldn't get any sense out of either of them. They just brushed me off with 'Not now, Ben' and 'She'll call you when she's back, OK?' then slammed the door in my face.

Something was definitely up, and I'd been too stupid and selfish to acknowledge it. If Aaron McAnally could shake my hand in public and apologise, I could pick up the phone and call my best friend and beg her to let me know she was OK.

So I did.

The phone went straight to voicemail, just like it had every other time I'd tried to call. I took a deep breath. 'Hi, Chelsea. It's me, Ben. So, I broke it off with Peter – which isn't even his real name, by the way. Anyway, I just want to say you were right, and I was wrong, and I'm an idiot. Look, I know something's not right, but your mum and dad won't tell me anything. They just slammed the door in my face, again. I don't care what kind of trouble you're in, just get in touch and let me know you're OK. And if you're not OK, well, get in touch and let me know that, too. I miss having you around, and if there's anything I can do to help, just say so. OK, Dad's calling me about taking the bins out or something, so I have to go. Please call me soon. I love you, you moron. Bye-bye.'

14

BEING DIFFERENT

J amie was hanging out in my bedroom, watching my video on YouTube.

'You were always one of those perfect kids,' she said, grabbing my pillow and propping herself up on it, so she could watch the video of Aaron and Killer one more time, 'who never did anything wrong. You always helped with the washing up. You always came top of the class at school. You always behaved yourself when we had visitors, and said please and thank you, and brushed your teeth before bed, and made me look like a right little brat.'

'But you were a little brat. That's not my fault. You were always chasing the boys around the yard, threatening to hit them with a baseball bat. Remember that?'

'Yeah, but that was ages ago. I was only a kid. I got nice and sensible and boring when I went to secondary school. I thought, well, I've got to be more like Ben. He doesn't run around getting into trouble, and Mum and Dad are always proud of him. I didn't know you had this evil streak underneath your ironed polo shirts and your colour-coordinated socks. You're, like, an evil genius.'

'I wish I'd been a bit more cheeky,' I said, blocking a guy on Grindr because his profile said he was already married. 'I was a bit of a goody-two-shoes, you know? I think it was because I knew I was gay, and I was afraid of disappointing everybody, so I made a special effort to be perfect.'

'Poor Aaron,' Jamie said, as she lay there flat on her stomach, kicking her new trainers in the air, idly scrolling through the comments section underneath the video. 'You have to feel a little bit sorry for him. Everyone thinks he's gross. Ha ha.'

'Don't feel too sorry for him,' I said, wondering why nobody in my area seemed to be around my age, single and reasonably cute. 'The school still has to have a meeting about whether I'm a bad influence on kids, thanks to him.'

'You'll be fine,' Jamie said. 'Mum would never let them away with firing you. Hey, you know what you said about acting good because you're gay? I used to worry about people thinking I was naughty because I'm black. Like, every time I got into trouble, they'd be like, well, what do you expect? And they'd sort of nod and raise an eyebrow as if to say *typical black girl*. So then you end up being twice as good, just to prove them wrong. It's stupid, isn't it? Because you're letting them win.'

'But you were never really naughty. You were just a kid.'

'Neither were you. You were just Ben, the perfect big brother.'

'It's nice to know we can be naughty, though. If someone really deserves it.'

'Yeah.'

I could feel summer just around the corner, in the way the leaves hung heavier on the trees, the butterflies were fluttering through our gardens, and the cats were making kittens. At school, the teachers were tired and the pupils were giddy. Boxes of fruit were stacked outside the greengrocer's, mums and grans picking up strawberries, raspberries and peaches for fruit salads. The flowers were fat and lush, the recycling bins were already beginning to stink in the heat, and lads from the estate were peeling off their shirts to drink cans in the afternoon, panned out in their yards, working on their sunburns. I wondered if I would do anything with my summer besides lie in my bedroom and flirt with lads online, or if I'd at least make it to a few parties with drag queens and dancers and students who were one year older and living away from home for the first time. Maybe I'd go drinking in the park with Soda and Gary, cans of cider stashed in brown paper bags, with mouldy-looking pigeons hobbling around our ankles. In my daydreams, Chelsea was back, punching me on the arm as I dribbled cider down my chin. She would scornfully tell the skinny topless lads that no one wanted to see their ribcages and their scrawny arms, and unwrap the sandwiches her mum had made us – cheese and ham in a French baguette, with a drizzle of the green pesto that she likes so much, and a bag of salty crisps and some homemade banana bread for afters. We'd feed the pigeons a few crumbs of cake then shoo them away, laughing at their scaldy toes and their stringy wings.

But Chelsea hadn't got back to me since I'd left her that voicemail, and Soda and Gary were too busy being a couple, so I was on my own.

'Hey, Ben?'

'What?'

'When did you know you were gay?'

Usually I hate that question. It's as if the person asking you is trying to figure you out, trying to discover this magical moment you had, when something clicked into place and everything made sense. It wasn't like that, but I didn't mind Jamie asking.

'Everyone else knew I was gay before I did,' I said.

'What do you mean?'

'When I went to school, everyone said I was a gay boy because I didn't like football, or I sang along to stupid pop songs with the girls, or whatever. And they were right, you know? Maybe they wouldn't have been right about everyone, but they were right about me. I didn't know it at the time, but it was there, and everyone else could see it.'

'When did you realise they were right?'

'There wasn't, like, one moment. I used to wish I wasn't gay just so the other kids would leave me alone. But I guess I started to have little crushes on guys when I was about ten or twelve … Silly things. Like I really liked Tony McAllister's hair, and I used to think about us hanging out together and holding hands. It sounds really stupid now.'

'Nah, it sounds cute. I bet you would've made a nice couple. You, with your top button tied up, and him, with his floppy blond hair and his tie all crooked to one side, holding hands.'

I remembered having my first wet dream about Tony McAllister. I'd woken up thinking I'd wet the bed, even though I'd felt sort of pleasantly dazed, but some things you just don't share with your sister.

'So how's that boy who likes you?' I said.

'Oh, you know,' Jamie said airily, rolling onto her back and putting her earphones in. 'He still likes me. But don't forget you promised not to tell Mum and Dad, OK?'

'OK,' I said, and poked Jamie with my foot to stop her rolling off the bed.

Jamie lay there listening to her girlbands, and I thought about how being gay can make you feel different than other people. You grow up feeling a bit like an alien, surrounded by so many boys and girls who seem, well, typical. They like the things they're supposed to like, and you like the things you're not supposed to like, and you either learn to feel OK with it, or you learn to hide it, to try to fit in. It makes you feel like a bad person, until you learn it's OK to be you. I hoped that growing up in a world where being gay was normal would mean, in the future, kids like me wouldn't have those nights alone in bed wishing they were someone else. I scrolled through my phone as Jamie sang along badly to her current favourite song.

I guess it wasn't such a bad thing that the internet replaced gay bars as the best place to meet potential new boyfriends. If I'd spent as much time in PantiBar as I did online, I would've been alcoholic and broke, as well as single.

I'd had enough of moping around, waiting for the summer to start. I decided the time was right to delete Grindr and make a new online profile. But where to start? Tinder, Gaydar, Gay Romeo, Manhunt, Fitlads, Recon, Jack'd, Scruff, OKCupid, Plenty of Fish, Hornet, Growlr, Bender, GuySpy …

I picked the least sleazy option and got to work, agreeing

that I was eighteen years of age, even though I wasn't yet. First of all, you had to say a little bit about yourself. But what were you supposed to say? How could you sum up your life in a couple of lines?

Hey, just a regular guy, I like nights outs with my friends and nights in with the TV and a bottle of wine. Even better with the right guy. Ha ha.

No, that was too bland.

Say hi. I don't bite, unless you like it ;)

Ugh, that was too cheesy.

Average guy looking for same. No drama, no issues, no closet cases.

That was probably true, but it sounded like I was really dull, with a troubled past.

Almost finished school ...

No, no, no, I'd get kicked off the site.

It was harder than it looked. I decided to be honest.

Nice guy with a happy life, looking for a decent guy without any big hang-ups, so we can eat pizza and play video games all night.

That about summed it up, in all its boring glory. Next, I had to say what my hobbies and interests were. That wasn't so bad, but Soda had taught me there were certain mistakes you had to avoid. If you said 'Lady Gaga!' or '*RuPaul's Drag Race*!!' or '*The*

X-Factor!!!' then loads of guys were going to skip over you. But then again, there was no point saying you liked football and guitar bands if you were actually into drag and only listened to the solo records of former girl-band members.

Well, it always paid to be upfront. If it worked for Soda, it could work for me.

Xbox 360 (if you like *Grand Theft Auto* we already get along), burger and chips with vanilla milkshake (now you know what to get me on a date), dancing badly with my friends (they all dance better than me), dumb horror movies where everyone dies one by one (I'd survive longer than you – fact), pondering the meaning of life (I'll get back to you on that, still working on it), oh, and I'm not averse to guys who like Lady Gaga or *RuPaul's Drag Race* (and if that's too gay, then get over it. I still hate *The X-Factor*, though).

Next were the easy questions about my height, weight, eye colour and hair colour, but the one I wasn't sure about was sexual position. I hadn't figured that out yet. I remembered Soda's advice, which he'd come up with after dating Bradley, an aspiring model who existed solely on herbal tea and Instagram likes. He was buff, he was blond and, after three months of passionate snogging but no actual action, it became apparent that they weren't compatible, so it was never going to happen.

'Trust me,' Soda had said, 'it might not be very politically correct to label yourself top or bottom, but it saves so much *time*.'

The truth was, I didn't know if I was a top or a bottom, so I hedged my bets and went with versatile, hoping to find out.

I was trying to find three photos that didn't make me look like a complete troll, when Chelsea walked in. It was completely typical that she didn't knock, just pushed open the door and stomped into the room as if she had a right to be there.

It was ages since I'd seen her, sure, but something was different. She'd changed, somehow. She wasn't slouching, for a start. She held her head up high, as if she was about to make an announcement, but then she spotted Jamie on the bed and sort of folded in on herself, resuming her usual slouching position.

I threw my phone aside and leapt up. I didn't care what had changed. I was just glad she was back. I was about to hug her, but I stopped. A tiny part of me was angry that she'd disappeared from my life for a second time without telling me why. I wanted the truth. 'Where the hell have you been?'

Chelsea looked at me, stunned. 'Mum and Dad didn't tell you?'

'No. Your mum and dad won't tell me anything. All they said was you were having a rest cure, whatever that means. Are you sick? Is it cancer? Did you do something stupid?'

Chelsea passed a hand over her face, her whole body shuddering. I thought for one horrible second that she'd broken down in tears, but then I heard the laughter bubble out of her, erupting in big snorts of mirth.

'Well, I don't know what's so funny,' I said. 'We have a massive row, you disappear, you suspend your Instagram account, you don't answer your phone, everyone acts like you're dead, and then you come back here and laugh in my face like it's all some sort of big joke. I don't think it's funny at all.'

'You're right,' said Chelsea, her laughter stopping abruptly. 'I just thought that being back would turn out differently.'

'I think I'll just … er … go charge this,' said Jamie, waving her phone, which was still blaring loudly. She looked back and forth from Chelsea to me, awkward and embarrassed, like when Granny and Granddad are having a row and no one knows where to look. I nodded.

Jamie ran to the door, then ran back. 'It's nice to have you back,' Jamie said, hugging Chelsea quickly then breaking away.

Chelsea ruffled Jamie's afro, and my little sister disappeared to her own bedroom.

It was just the two of us, face to face.

Maybe Jamie was listening in. Maybe Mum and Dad were straining to hear our voices through the living-room ceiling. Maybe Mr and Mrs Nealon had their ears pressed to the walls of Chelsea's bedroom, trying to catch what we had to say through the walls of our houses. It didn't matter. Everyone could listen in, even if we had nothing to say to each other. We stood in silence, and I tried to work out how exactly Chelsea looked different.

As I looked her up and down, she stood tall and let me look. She'd lost weight, mostly from her chest, which looked flatter now. Her face was not exactly gaunt, but you could see her cheekbones, slicing her face on either side, her straight black brows frowning over deep brown eyes that looked calmer than I'd seen them in a while. Her skin was milky pale, smudged with just a hint of blue beneath the eyes, as if she hadn't been sleeping very well. I'm bad at noticing haircuts, but even I could see she'd had her hair cropped short, tight around the sides and just a little tangled on top. She had a cigarette tucked behind one ear, as usual. She was wearing black combat trousers and boots – no skinny jeans for Chelsea – and a checked shirt over the whole lot.

'I like the haircut,' I said. 'Usually your hair is all over your face, like you're trying to hide something.'

'Maybe I was,' Chelsea said, sticking out her lip to blow a stray strand of her fringe back from her eyes. 'But I'm not any more.'

I put my head to one side and looked at her face.

'Is it your ears?' I said. 'Mum's ears stick out at slightly different angles, so she never crops her hair real short. She's paranoid about them. I always think she should worry more about the tacky earrings she wears – you know, the ones that look like enormous hula-hoops, or the ones in the shape of fruit – but there's no talking to her. Your ears stick out a bit, don't they? I've never really noticed before. It's kind of cute.'

'Shut up, Ben.'

'Sorry. I'm nervous. I can't stop talking when I'm nervous.'

'Believe me,' Chelsea said, 'I'm more nervous than you are.'

But I didn't understand what she was talking about, because she looked perfectly calm. She looked the calmest I'd ever seen her. Usually Chelsea stomps around being angry, kicking cans out of her way in the street, knocking over pint glasses left on windowsills just to watch them shatter on the ground, throwing an apple from hand to hand like a grenade instead of actually eating it, always alive with nervous energy, but now, she just stood there, perfectly still, as if she wanted me to see her, really see her, for the first time. As if she'd made up her mind to be there, in front of me, after being away for so long. As if she had something important to say.

'Why?' I said.

I shoved my hands in my pockets in case they were shaking, preparing myself for the worst. She was dying. She was dying of something that couldn't be cured. Or she'd tried to end her own life, because I wasn't enough for her, nobody was, and the voices in her head saying she should end it all were stronger than our friendship, stronger than our love, and one day, soon, she would do it. She would take a bunch of pills, and they wouldn't be dog laxatives, and that would be the end of Chelsea. I fought an insane urge to laugh.

'I didn't want to tell you like this,' Chelsea said. 'Mum and Dad were supposed to tell you. I asked them to. When I went to see the doctor, I said, make sure you tell Ben, because he's going to be worried, and he might even think it's his fault, because that's the kind of loveable dope he is, always thinking he can rescue other people. But Mum and Dad have had a hard time adjusting to everything, so I guess they never found the right words to say.'

'Look,' I said desperately, 'whatever it is, doctors can help. They cure cancer. They cure cancer nearly all the time. Or, I don't know, whatever it is you have. Is it HIV? It doesn't matter, Chelsea. There are treatments you can get these days, it's not a life sentence any more. And if it's – if you're having dark thoughts, I don't know, if you tried to kill yourself, I'm there for you, OK? I'm sorry, I know I'm saying this all wrong. I just want you to know that it's not as bad as you think. I'm here, Chelsea. I'll always be here, no matter what. You know that, right?'

'It's nothing like that.'

'Oh, bloody hell. I've been so stupid. You're pregnant, aren't you? Did you go for an abortion? You can tell me. I'm pro-choice. Nobody minds these –'

'I'm a boy,' said Chelsea, her voice faltering just a little.

I stared at her, waiting for the punchline, but none came.

'I'm a boy,' Chelsea said, stronger this time.

I didn't know what to say.

'The chances of me ever getting pregnant are, like, zero,' Chelsea said. 'I was born in a girl's body, but I'm getting that fixed. I've spoken to doctors and psychiatrists and social workers, you name it, but I know who I am. That's why I dropped out of Transition Year, to see a whole load of doctors, but they said I was too young to go through any changes yet. But I'm older now, and I'm still a boy, and the quicker my body matches my identity, the better, as far as I'm concerned. So, nope. No kids. And I'm not called Chelsea any more.'

I collapsed on my bed and sank my face into my hands. 'Oh, thank God,' I said. 'I thought it was going to be something bad.'

'I don't think you understand,' Chelsea said. 'I'm a boy.'

I looked up and grinned. 'I get it, you idiot. You're trans. So what? You're not dead. You don't have cancer, or HIV, and you haven't tried to kill yourself.'

Chelsea sat down on the bed beside me. 'You – you don't mind?'

'Are you kidding? I'm ecstatic. You're alive. You're – you're *you.*'

'It's not that simple,' Chelsea said, looking at her hands. 'I mean, Chelsea is gone. The Chelsea you know, the Chelsea you're friends with, she – she never really existed. It's not as simple as changing your clothes and calling yourself a different name. There's hormone therapy, there's psychological therapy, there's surgery, eventually.'

'Start at the beginning,' I said. 'What do I call you?'

'Charles,' said Charles. 'That's my name. Or Charlie to my friends.'

'We're blokes. We call each other buddies.'

And that's when I threw my arms around my new, old buddy, and suddenly my face was wet, and I felt like such a sap for crying, because I was so relieved to have her back, even if she was a he.

'Whoa. What are you crying for?'

'I'm not crying,' I said, wiping my face on the back of my sleeve. 'My face is just randomly leaking for no reason, that's all.'

'You idiot,' Charlie said, and punched me on the arm, and that's when I saw him, really saw him, for the first time. His sculpted lips, and his deep brown, scornful eyes, and the way his ears stuck out under a tumble of black curls. I knew what I'd been missing all this time, and I knew that it had been here, under my nose, for as long as I could remember. The thing was, it had been in disguise, but now the secret was out, Charlie was out, and he was sitting there on the edge of my bed, where he'd always been, when we'd eaten takeaway pizza and played video games and fallen asleep with cigarettes smouldering in beer cans.

I guess that's what coming out is. A part of a person that they always tried to hide is lit up, and the bit that you'd always wondered about, the bit that was hidden away, suddenly makes sense.

Charlie was a guy.

In fact, Charlie was my kind of guy.

'Hey,' I said, and brushed away the stray strand of hair that kept falling in his eyes. 'I missed you.'

'I missed you too, buddy,' Charlie said, and I kissed him – yeah, *him* – on the lips, and felt him resist, then stop resisting, and kiss me back, and the bedroom began to spin, but that was OK, because everything felt right.

'Well,' Charlie said when we'd finally stopped kissing, and the bedroom stopped spinning, and he'd pulled his cigarette out from behind his ear and lit up. 'I guess this gives a whole new meaning to Transition Year, right?'

'Oh my God,' I said, hitting him with my pillow. 'That was so rehearsed.'

'Dude,' Charlie said, putting his free hand to the nape of my neck, and pulling my face close to his, so the only thing between us was the smoke on his breath, 'I've been rehearsing this my whole life.'

15

THE MEANING
OF LOVE

I t took Mr and Mrs Nealon a longer time to come around to the idea that they had a son, not a daughter. I'm not going to lie, though – I think the fact that Charlie and I became a couple helped them through it. They'd always secretly hoped that Chelsea and I would get together – you know, the slightly awkward girl meeting the ordinary boy next door. Me being gay ruined their plans, but their not-so-pretty daughter becoming their rather handsome son made it sort of OK again. Charlie went through a phase of trying to get rid of all the photos of him as a girl, but Mrs Nealon insisted on keeping them in a box, which she only took out when he wasn't around, to grieve for the daughter that was gone, while Charlie got on with the messy business of becoming a man. The family was in counselling, and it was helping Charlie's parents a whole lot.

Dad was cooking a barbecue for everyone in our back garden. 'Just to be neighbourly,' he said, but it was really to welcome Charlie into the family.

We stood there holding hands and grinning goofily while Mrs Nealon made straight for the white wine, and Mr Nealon talked about the latest football match with Jamie, and Dad gave Mum a hand with lifting the plates and cutlery, because she doesn't like to admit she can't manage with her lousy arm. Then he gave her a peck on the cheek, and she began to circulate around the other neighbours we'd invited.

'Jude and Sandra, how's the little one doing? Hey, Tony, it's nice to see you looking so well. Alison, don't get tipsy and mow someone down with that wheelchair ...'

'Barbecues,' Charlie whispered in my ear, 'freak me the hell out. They're like a throwback to when we all lived in caves and cooked outdoors. There's a reason we invented kitchens. Either shoot me or get me another cold beer.'

'Never change,' I said, kissing my boyfriend on the lips.

I went to get us a couple of cans as Charlie scrunched his empty one in his fist in a way that made my heart soar. I pointed to the recycling bin, and he pitched it in perfectly without even trying.

Granny and Granddad arrived in their battered old car,

parking haphazardly on the kerb. Granny always drives the car as if she's driving the tractor.

'Here comes trouble,' Mum said, handing her glass of wine to Jamie, who sniffed it, made a face, took a sip when she thought no one was looking, and promptly spat it out onto the grass. Mum fluffed around Granny and Granddad, finding them a seat and pressing hot-dogs on paper plates into their hands.

'Don't go giving him a beer,' Granny said. 'He promised to drive us home.'

'One beer won't hurt,' Granddad said. 'Sure I couldn't be any worse a driver than you, beer or no beer.'

'Didn't I get us here in one piece?' Granny said, biting into her hot-dog.

'That sausage would take the false teeth clean out of your head,' Granddad said. 'It's pure rubber. I'll be chewing on this all day. I need something to help wash it down.'

'You know you're not supposed to drink,' Mum said.

I grabbed an extra beer for Granddad, took Charlie by the hand and dragged him over to where Granny and Granddad were sitting.

'Are you sure this is a good idea?' Charlie said.

'Come on. We have to do it sometime.'

'But they're so old! I don't think they'll really get it.'

'Too late now. Here you go, Granddad,' I said. 'You might as well have one beer. This is Charlie. You've met before.'

'I was Chelsea then,' said Charlie.

Granddad looked Charlie up and down suspiciously, but took the beer. Charlie cracked open his can with his free hand and took a sip. They silently measured each other up.

'You're the young fella who used to be a girl, aren't you?'

'That's right.'

'And a fine handsome fella he is too,' said Granny, beaming. 'You look much happier now you're a boy, Chelsea.'

'Charlie,' I said.

'That's what I meant,' Granny said, munching on her hot-dog enthusiastically.

Granddad cracked open his beer and took a sip. I held on tighter to Charlie's hand. He gave my hand a squeeze back, and I knew that he was OK.

'And are yous allowed to hold hands now these days?'

'We could get married if we wanted to,' I said.

'How was the drive up?' Mum said brightly, but a little desperately.

'Awful as usual,' Granny said. 'I don't know why yous want to live in Dublin at all.'

'Sure, this is where all the modern people live,' Granddad said. 'The blacks and the gays and the people like Charlie here.

Isn't that right, Ben? Well, I'm not very modern, but then, your granny and me fell in love an awful long time ago.'

'We were just lucky,' said Granny, 'but the people have to make their own luck these days, don't they?'

'That's right,' Granddad said, nodding. 'So the best of luck to you both. Things have changed, but I suppose things have to change. And sure didn't Marie's second marriage turn out all right in the end?'

'Finally!' Mum said.

'Got enough food?' Dad said, appearing at Mum's side with a plateful of hot-dogs. 'The burgers are almost done.'

Jamie ran up and stole a hot-dog off the plate. 'Chewy,' she said. 'Hi, Granny, hi, Granddad. How's the farm? Are there any new lambs? Dad says lambs taste best with mint sauce, but I like the way they jump around in the field.'

'I'm not sure about these sausages, Nathan,' said Granddad. 'I'd better have another one, just to make up my mind.'

'Make sure you get plenty of mustard and onions – that's the secret to a good hot-dog.'

'Well now, isn't that awful fancy?'

'You boys go off and enjoy yourselves,' Granny said, as Jamie sat on her knee.

'They're so boring, Granny,' Jamie said, rolling her eyes. 'All they do is play video games. Can I come and visit the farm?'

'Well, of course you can,' Granny said, 'as long as you're willing to do some good hard work when you're there. A farm doesn't run itself, you know …'

'Come on,' Charlie said, tugging me by the hand. 'Let's mingle.'

But before we could mingle, Miss Murgatroyd arrived in a cloud of floating floral scarves. I could see her making a bee-line for me, so I tucked my can of beer under one arm, poured her a glass of wine, and steered her to the other side of the garden, with Charlie in tow. She sipped her wine daintily, her eyes shining with good news.

'I've just spoken to the board of management, Ben,' she said, 'and I'm delighted to tell you they've dismissed the complaint against you. It's the opinion of the school that your work has been exemplary and the complaint unfounded.'

'Thanks!' I said, and surprised myself by throwing my arms around her, almost spilling wine everywhere. Even with everything else that had been going on, I'd been worrying about the complaint. This meant there'd be no problem going on to study teacher training in college. Already, there was talk about fixing the law that prevented teachers being out at school. There'd also been a change in the law for trans people.

'Speaking of good news,' Miss Murgatroyd said, 'I've heard you'll be allowed to update your birth certificate to reflect your true gender, Charles. Congratulations. You can go to college as the young man you were always meant to be.'

'Yeah,' Charlie said, 'if I get the points. If I don't, I'll blame Ben. I'll tell everyone those notes he gave me weren't good enough.'

'I'm sure you'll do just as well as Ben!' Miss Murgatroyd beamed.

Dad was circling the garden with another plate of food. 'Burgers are served!' he said, presenting us each with a slab of dead cow.

Miss Murgatroyd looked at the plate queasily. 'Perhaps just a slice of cheese … on a bun … with a piece of lettuce …'

'Vegetarian,' I mouthed, and Dad scowled. He's totally cool with gay and trans people, but vegetarians turning down good food gets on his nerves.

'Let me top you up there, Jenny,' Mum said, coming to the rescue and filling Miss Murgatroyd's glass to the brim, 'and Nathan will rustle up a nice cheese and tomato sandwich for you.'

'Well, maybe just one more glass,' Miss Murgatroyd said. 'It's been a very trying year … Ah, so nice to see Jamie making friends outside of school.'

Charlie and I exchanged a knowing glance as a boy grabbed Jamie by the arm, dragged her off Granny's knee, and they disappeared behind the rose bush. Mr Nealon threw back his beer, waved cheerfully in our direction and went to help turn the chicken on the barbecue as Dad sorted a sandwich for Miss Murgatroyd.

I leaned my head on Charlie's shoulder. 'We might even go to the same college,' I said.

'Holding hands in the canteen,' Charlie said.

'Pissing off all the bigots,' I said.

'Ben?' Charlie said. 'You're not just doing this because I'm one of your projects?'

'Don't be daft,' I said. 'I love you because you're manly, and handsome, and we're best friends. I know we haven't figured out all the sexy stuff yet. So what? We can work up to that. I wasn't ready for it anyway. If you can wait for me, I can wait for you. And in the meantime, we'll just get to know each other. As lads, I mean.'

'Cool,' Charlie said. 'Oh. My. God. Did you know Soda was arriving in drag?'

Miss Ugg Lee made an entrance just as one of the neighbours got the speakers working and an Abba song burst into life. The good news was Soda had finally got rid of the boots and opted for high heels. The bad news was high heels didn't work on our lawn. She got three steps in and fell over with a splat. Gary just pointed and laughed, his big belly wobbling as his boyfriend stood up, kicked off his heels and said, 'Who needs footwear anyway? I just need a drink!'

Mr Nealon pressed a can of beer in each of their hands, and they joined us as we munched our burgers.

'I'm famished,' Gary said, clinking cans all round. 'Where's the grub?'

'You're not a vegetarian, are you?' Dad said, appearing at his elbow and staring at him suspiciously.

'Do I look vegetarian?' Gary said, helping himself to the entire plateful of burgers. 'Soda doesn't eat when he's in drag, so I get his share too. Win!'

'I'm glad someone likes his grub,' Dad said, and smacked Gary's belly.

'Beer is fattening enough,' Soda said, chugging back half a can. 'We have to work off the calories later, with plenty of vigorous –'

'*Soda,*' Charlie and I said in unison.

'– dancing to Abba,' Soda said. 'Maybe just one bite of your burger, darling.'

Everything was cool. A light shower a mile or so away twinkled over the rooftops but didn't even cloud our back yard. We ate, and drank, and a double-rainbow appeared just above our village, which couldn't have been planned any better.

I looked around at all our friends and neighbours and felt a warm glow, although something, or someone, was missing. It was too perfect. I held on tight to Charlie's hand and tried to work out who or what was nagging at the back of my mind.

A guy's head appeared above our garden wall.

'Killer!' Darren screeched, pointing at Charlie. 'Attack!'

Killer leapt over the garden wall and made straight for Charlie.

Dad threw his burger to the ground and ran for the dog.

Gary's mouth hung open, staring at Darren's evil grin.

I let go of Charlie's hand and felt my fists clench.

Charlie knelt down and said, 'Here, girl!' as Killer bounded up to him, covering his face in slobbery kisses.

'No!' Darren screeched. 'You're doing it all wrong, you dumb dog!'

'Ah, shut up,' Aaron said, running up behind him and grabbing him by the arm. 'You're making a show of us! Here, Chelsea, I'm sorry about that.'

'It's Charles now,' Wayne said, appearing behind his mates, out of breath. 'Keep up, you dopes.'

'Right, right,' Aaron said. 'Eh, just drop the dog over whenever you get a chance, OK? Later.'

You could tell it was a bit weird for him, but he was trying, and that was what mattered.

'Sure,' I said, as his mates dragged Darren off, Dad fed his ruined burger to Killer, and Charlie tickled the dog's ears.

My phone beeped, and I dragged it out of my pocket. Unknown number.

Fancy a bit of this?

A dick pic from Thomas, of course.

Some guys never get the message.

I knelt down in the grass beside Charlie as he tickled Killer's tummy, and held my phone at arm's length. Gary and Soda leaned in, their arms around each other, and grinned. Charlie, who was all man whatever was currently in his pants, who loved me as passionately as I loved him, who smoked too many cigarettes and drank too much beer and would have to earn his stubble, and his street cred, and his place in the world, but who could always rely on me being there by his side as we navigated the world of masculinity together, hand in hand, whatever other people thought of us, kissed me as I took the snap and sent it back to Thomas.

This is what love looks like.

AUTHOR'S NOTE

The idea for this book first came to me when I was sitting in a pub in London with my good friend Colin, who wanted to read 'a gay story with a happy ending'. We were wondering why LGBTQ fiction always took so long to catch up with LGBTQ reality. From the perspective of two Northern Irish gay men who'd been teenagers in the 1990s, there was plenty to be happy about. Things had improved for us and for millions of other people too, thanks to the activism of those from the generations before us. We'd witnessed a sea change in popular culture, where the LGBTQ experience had gone from being unmentionable to being celebrated, and we were grateful.

When I'd first started writing, it was important to me to give gay male characters a voice in Irish fiction. This was considered niche, and probably still is. Increasingly, as the gay experience crossed over from being seen as something edgy and cool into the mainstream, that sense of urgency faded a little. There were gay storylines on Netflix, there were out gay popstars for teenagers to look up to, and drag queens had stepped out of the club and onto TV, becoming recognised as a mainstream cultural phenomenon. All those things were part of the progress we'd all wanted – so why did it feel like gay fiction wasn't keeping up?

We both agreed that when you looked a little closer there were still some stories that weren't being told. We'd had the coming-out stories, we'd had the rejected-by-society stories, we'd had the tragic love stories that always ended in death, so what was next? Where were the LGBTQ friendship groups and supportive parents? Where were the amateur drag queens and working-class kids? Where were all the people of colour?

And that was when I decided to write a book for Colin, with a happy, well-adjusted main character, one whose friends and family weren't all from the same background, one who would discover that his best friend was trans, and that was great.

As LGBTQ people, we need to see ourselves in stories. In a world that is mostly straight, we need to make ourselves visible to show that our experiences, our friendships and our love lives matter every bit as much as other people's. One book cannot be all things to all people. It can't represent everyone – even if it tried to, it couldn't. But by telling our stories, one at a time, we add a little piece to the rainbow tapestry of the LGBTQ experience.

When I started writing this book, the same-sex marriage referendum had just passed in Ireland by popular vote, but not before some ugly discourse played out in public. Drag queen and accidental activist Panti Bliss helped put the issue in the forefront of the national consciousness, so I figured no post-referendum book would be complete without a well-deserved cameo.

By the time I was in the middle of writing this book, the Gender Recognition Act was passed in Ireland, enabling all trans people to have full legal recognition of their preferred gender. Our country decided it was the right thing to do for an often vulnerable minority of people, who deserve the right to go about their lives without being harassed for who they are.

Since I finished writing this book, some more ugly discourse has played out in public, particularly around trans rights. But you know what? Ireland is still Ireland, with marriage rights for same-sex couples, gender recognition for trans people, and the sky hasn't fallen down. Keep looking up, and you'll find that rainbows are going strong.

So with gratitude to the generations of LGBTQ activists who've gone before, this book is dedicated to Colin, with thanks to Panti, and for all the teenagers of today.

Jarlath Gregory